Where You Live

stories

Also by Andrew Roe

The Miracle Girl

WHERE YOU LIVE

stories

ANDREW ROE

Engine Books
Indianapolis

Engine Books
PO Box 44167
Indianapolis, IN 46244
enginebooks.org

Some of the stories included here have appeared, sometimes in slightly different form, in the following publications: "Close" in *PANK*; "The Gift" in *The Cincinnati Review*; "America's Finest City" in *One Story*; "Are You Okay?" in *Tin House;* "Renters" (published as "Please Don't Tell Me That"), "A Matter of Twenty-Four Hours," and "Rough" in *Glimmer Train* ("Rough" also appeared in the anthology *Where Love Is Found: 24 Tales of Connection*); "Job History" in *The Dr. T.J. Eckleburg Review*; "Solo Act" in *Opium*; "Why We Came to Target at 9:58 on a Monday Night" in *Freight Stories;* "The Big Empty" in *Sententia;* "My Status" in *Slice;* "Where Shall We Meet?" in *Used Furniture Review;* "Where You Live" in *The Good Men Project;* "The Boyfriend" in *Storyglossia;* "Mexico" in *Failbetter;* "Burn" in *Avery Anthology;* "The Riot and Rage That Love Brings" in *Kenyon Review Online;* and "Stalling" in *SmokeLong Quarterly.*

ISBN: 978-1-938126-43-7

Library of Congress Control Number: 2017938070

to Maria

Never tell them where it hurts.
—Richard Buckner

CONTENTS

CLOSE

CLOSE

AN OLDER MAN AND a younger man, the latter mentioning a woman with a kid and prescriptions for multiple medications, the former then offering relationship advice, saying, "Don't get too close," the latter then nodding and agreeing and saying, "I know, I know. I'll try. I won't."

THE GIFT

THE GIFT

THE PREMONITIONS STARTED NOT long after Shell took one of those home pregnancy tests—plus you are, minus you're not—and sure enough, it was plus. But instead of the bright and shiny happy couples that inhabit the TV commercials for such products, we were in the mildewed bathroom, confronted with our sagging, shrugging selves in the mirror, yelling at each other and calling for a redo.

"Don't we have another test somewhere?" Shell demanded to know. Her eyes were as wide and as open as I'd ever seen them, and once again she held up the little tube thing to the light. One of the bathroom bulbs had burned out and hadn't been replaced.

"No, we don't," I said.

"Are you sure?"

I didn't answer right away. Because I wasn't sure. That's a good solid rule of thumb, especially for men, but also women, too, I guess: never answer right away if you're not sure of something. You might get in trouble later.

"No," I admitted at some point.

"Then check, why don't you."

I checked. Nothing in the medicine cabinet but floss and tweezers and rust.

"Okay then," said Shell, who had already gnawed away part of one fingernail and was diligently working on a second. "Let's do this. Let's go to the store and get another one. Best two out of three. We drive to the store—no, *you* drive to the store and *I* stay here and work on another pee sample."

She hiked up her skirt, began to squat.

"Look," I started, then stopped. I was on the verge of going off on Shell, how she can't handle the dramatic, make-or-break moments of life, but I ceased. I desisted. Now wasn't the time.

"Let's be calm and try and look at this rationally," I advised, aiming for the reassuring tone of a sedate, lab-coated scientist; I would have stroked my beard if I'd had one.

"Take a step back," I thoughtfully continued. "Deep breath. Get some perspective. I mean really, think about it—how scientific can it be if you can buy the goddamn thing at Thrifty's?"

Shell, however, was not swayed.

"Ninety-seven percent," she countered. "Ninety-seven percent accuracy rate. Those are pretty good, like, odds."

"Says who?"

"Says Johnson & Johnson, says so right here on the box." Shell retrieved the soothingly colored package from the trash can and flattened it against my chest, evidence. "What are we going to do, Rick?" she raged.

"I don't know what we're going to do," I said. "I'm thinking. We need to think about this."

And on and on. With each passing minute, the tiny bathroom seemed to get tinier and tinier. Stuff was accumulating in there. Eventually it got to the point where the two of us couldn't breathe or speak. At last Shell stormed out and cracked open a bottle of peppermint schnapps that I hadn't even known we had, and then proceeded to pour it down the kitchen sink when she remembered that she was ninety-seven percent sure she was pregnant. All in all, then, not exactly a glossy Kodak moment suitable for framing, I admit. Not exactly a scene you'd want to share when your kid asks about the first time you became aware of the miracle that it is/was his/her existence. And so you see: how the lying, the revising of the past, begins.

At the time we'd been living together off and on (and off) for close to a year (a year!), with the usual ups and downs and periods of unremarkable in-betweens. Hardly a stable situation, though, what with our tempers and suspicions and precarious employment, not to mention Shell's semi-seeing this other guy, Ramón Something, and me still spending way too much time at El Torito's happy hour. But finally, late one night after the home pregnancy test standoff and after one of our famous reconciliatory lays and while passing a soggy post-coital pint of Ben and Jerry's back and forth, Shell and I vetoed an abortion and agreed to try to really make it work this time. Really. We were both pushing thirty and vaguely wondering what would become of ourselves if we stayed single for much longer. Friends were either married or heavily coupled, or in the process of getting heavily coupled. Birth announcements and shower invitations arrived in the mail with an alarming regularity. Life was happening. It seemed like it was time—or that time would soon pass us by if we didn't take some kind of appropriate action.

Our lives jumped into warp speed after that. We made promises, consolidated our CDs and books, ordered return address stickers with both our names. No longer did we close the door when doing our respective business in the bathroom. We even got married. For the kid. For the future—*our future.* That's the way it was now. A whole new way of thinking would be required. As for the wedding itself, well, it was a quickie affair, there's no other way to put it. Shell broke one of her heels and had to go down the aisle barefoot. Her mother cried. Shell cried. Most everyone got too drunk, including the sunglasses-wearing D.J., "Funk Master Doug," which led to grumbling and complaints about everything, most notably the anorexic food portions and the lack of air conditioning. Marlon, my best man, a friend from high school who still lived at home and sold historical Time-Life videos on the phone, gave a speech that sounded like it was in Russian. After ten minutes someone told him to shut up. Then Marlon cried. One of the flower girls found a dead bug in her scalloped potatoes.

For the honeymoon we drove seven hours to the Grand Canyon, stepped out of the car, looked at it, unimpressed, it's a giant hole in the ground. On the way out we stopped in a gift shop, figuring we should probably buy a key chain or something to commemorate the occasion, and Shell found this one book called *Death on the Rim,* which was all about how people fall into it, the canyon, or are pushed, murdered, usually by a husband or a wife. Apparently the Grand Canyon was a good spot to get rid of an unwanted spouse. Happened all the time. Shell rattled off the grim statistics as we climbed into the car, having settled on a shot glass as our one and only purchase. Then it was seven more hours of desert and numbing flatness and we were back in our apartment in San Diego. That was when Shell had the first major premonition, on the drive home, somewhere near Barstow: my sister's kid Nathan was a fish. More specifically, he was a fish out of water who couldn't breathe and was struggling for life.

When we got home there was a message on the answering machine. Shell's cat Hiccup had pissed all over the sofa again, and as I picked him up to show him the error of his free-form urinating ways, Shell hit the button and we heard my sister frantically rambling like she used to do back when she was more or less permanently coked out and dating this ex-pro football player no one had ever heard of. She ranted about Nathan and how he almost died and he was having this fit and he couldn't breathe and it was fucking horrible and she was freaking out but had enough sense to call 9-1-1 and the ambulance came and he was okay now, he was in the hospital, he was okay, but he was an epileptic, did we know what that meant? And if we didn't just for our own information it had to do with the nervous system, and she'd never thought of herself as religious but now she was wondering if she was, and maybe I should get checked out or something because she was pretty sure it was hereditary—epilepsy, that is, not religion.

"So he *was* squirming like a fish," Shell said, pretending that the familiar cloud of cat piss hanging in the air wasn't really there. "It was a seizure. That's what it was. That's what I saw."

Hiccup bolted out of my hands and disappeared down the dark hallway, defiant in that universal defiant-cat way. On the kitchen table there was mail, bills, newspapers—obligations I didn't want to deal with yet. It was our honeymoon, after all.

"What's this?"

The landlady, Mrs. Tokuda, had slipped an envelope under the door. I recognized her handwriting immediately, the kind of pristine schoolgirl penmanship that doesn't seem humanly possible. We're too flawed, too damaged of a species for such perfection.

"What's it say?" asked Shell.

"Don't you know?"

"I'm predicting bad news."

I opened it. The letter said that due to rising maintenance costs our rent would be increased the following month. And P.S.: Congratulations! Have a happy marriage and wonderful life together! Mrs. Tokuda added several more exclamation points for emphasis. She was a sweet, tiny, almost miniature woman who as a child had been put in one of those Japanese internment camps during World War II. Somewhere in Wyoming, I think. Whenever she raised the rent or took a long time to fix the toilet it was always hard to get mad or make a fuss.

"Right again," I confirmed.

"Maybe I should go on TV," Shell said.

"Maybe."

"I got the tits."

"You sure do. We could make money off those tits. They're professional, you know."

Then Shell stared at the empty living room wall, that prominent space where we'd always meant to hang something, uh, prominent. It was one of our greatest failures as a couple, that space, and we'd stopped talking about it. What she was thinking now, I didn't know. She looked a little lost, like she might have walked into the wrong apartment by mistake. But also maybe almost happy, staring like that. The slightest, smallest hint of a smile. The world in repose, awaiting her next move. I didn't want to say anything to break the spell or whatever it was.

"Let's call Lydia tomorrow," she said. "It sounds like Nathan's all right. It's late. I'm exhausted. I'm not even going to shower. I smell like Taco Bell."

The wedding, the marathon drive, the fast food—it had all caught up to us. Like an old married couple, we helped each other into the bedroom, kicked Hiccup off the bed, and laid down, too tired for sex, too tired to talk or even acknowledge this momentous event: our first night at home as husband and wife. We slept in until noon, swearing that we'd stay in bed all day, talking about room service and what we'd order if we could: poached eggs, sourdough toast, bacon, coffee, lots of coffee, mimosas. But by two o'clock or so we were up and about. Let's face it: Life doesn't stop like you sometimes wish it would. Not for us, not for anybody. Anyway, Shell jumped in the shower. I searched the fridge and cabinets for food, found nothing remotely edible except creamed corn and frozen taquitos, then admitted defeat as the hunter-gatherer of the household. I called for a pizza. Shell started doing her nails and a crossword, her hair still wet and smelling of that expensive herbal shampoo she uses even though she keeps saying we can't afford it. I got the money ready for the pizza, plus the coupon. The TV was on, too. We were married. There was paperwork, documentation. And yet nothing much seemed to have changed.

In the beginning it was mostly simple things: weather, football games, movie endings, celebrity breakups, when the phone was about to ring, who would stop by unexpectedly. Apparently being pregnant led to some sort of superior form of Zen consciousness. That was Shell's theory. She was on a higher frequency now. Mother frequency. But then, when she began throwing up and getting depressed and all grumped out, she'd have her doubts. This was hell. This was torture and fuck you all. That meant me.

Still the premonitions continued. She predicted that Hiccup would get sick. Two days later he was practically unconscious. We rushed him to the vet. After four hundred dollars of tests, we learned that he had advanced diabetes (which explained all the pissing) and would require insulin shots for the rest of his life. No more than a week later, Shell was boiling spaghetti, humming some doo-wop song about being true to your guy no matter what, and she said our neighbor Phil was in pain. The next day we saw Phil weeping by the swamp-like swimming pool (which everyone in the building was afraid to use, for pretty obvious reasons), saying that the frozen yogurt company he worked for had gone belly-up, Chapter 11. "No one eats frozen yogurt anymore," he wailed in a street preacher's urgent rasp. His breath smelled of beer and bad nachos. It was probably ninety degrees, noon, and he sat sprawled out in a neglected chaise lounge fully clothed, sweating like Shaquille O'Neal in the final minutes of the fourth quarter. Redness bloomed around his cheeks and forehead. "Remember frozen yogurt? Remember how it almost tasted as good as ice cream? It was revolutionary, man. But people don't remember. *They just don't remember a goddamned thing.*" We consoled Phil as best we could, convincing him to go inside before he became too sunburned.

Back in the apartment, Shell said, "I think I'm onto something here."

Those first months of the pregnancy we settled into what I guess was our new routine. Every day we checked Shell's stomach for signs of the baby, searching like archaeologists for any evidence of the mysterious life growing below, and yes, we did all that stupid stuff like talking to the baby and playing classical music to make it a genius. Winter came, which in San Diego isn't winter at all. It's just a name change—November, December, January. We endured the holidays, rented obscene amounts of movies and basically stayed in, arguing about names and methods of child rearing. I was more stern, spare the rod and all that, whereas Shell thought spanking was a form of child abuse. She favored time-outs and other enlightened modern practices.

"Were you ever spanked?" she asked me one morning as I was chipping away at the latest glacier that had formed in our freezer, which was supposed to defrost automatically but did not. Another of the apartment's many faults that we didn't complain to Mrs. Tokuda about.

"Hell yes," I said, sounding almost proud, which wasn't what I'd intended. I gave the frozen block another good whack with the ice pick. "Spanked, whipped, hit, slapped, knuckle rapped, you name it."

"Then congratulations," said Shell. "You were an abused child."

Even though I thought that was crap I let it go, kept on with the ice pick like I didn't care. Getting spanked, being put in your place, encountering power and authority beyond yourself—that was all part of growing up, of learning about the world and how to live in it. But they say compromise is important in a marriage—they do say that, don't they?—and I was doing my best, making the agreed-upon effort. When the time came for the ultrasound we didn't need it. "It's a boy," announced Shell, and of course she was right. But we went anyway, just to be sure, and because that's what you do these days. We asked the doctor if being pregnant had anything to do with being psychic. He had a Magnum P.I. mustache and wire-rimmed glasses that were supposed to make him look not just rich but cultured, too. We waited, but he didn't answer our question, just handed us the picture, mumbled something about the wonders of the human fetus, and said it was a boy. He circled the penis to verify.

We taped the ultrasound picture on the refrigerator next to the magnets and funny pictures we cut out of newspapers and magazines, and there it hung until I made a crack about how it was reassuring that the baby looked like me and not like Ramón. Then Shell tore it up. She tore it up into little eggshell pieces and then she tore up everything else on the fridge, including that priceless picture of Nixon and Elvis that has graced several different refrigerators over the years. She marched into the living room, livid, grabbed the closest object (it was a Blockbuster video, *Remains of the Day*, Shell's choice, not mine) and hurled it at me. She missed, but it hit the wall and exploded, bits of plastic and tape everywhere. It cost us something like a hundred bucks. The clerk couldn't explain to me why one measly videotape was so expensive. "Policy," he said, and how do you argue with that?

And so there were the occasional fights, commotions, communication blackouts, etc., and once or twice I left for a few days and then came back and it would be tense for a day, maybe two, tops, but then it would be all right. Nothing more than the usual. The time passed painlessly enough. By the sixth month Shell was rapidly getting bigger and bigger and she grumbled about how her body was like an inflatable toy, only she couldn't let out the air. She consumed massive amounts of TV, way more than the average 6.5 hours per day or whatever the latest statistic is. I was always bringing home movies, ice cream, magazines, new Nintendo games. Money-wise, Shell's unemployment wouldn't run out for another few months, and I picked up two or three night shifts a week at the printers, watching the giant machines spit out our local newspaper and drinking Jolt cola to stay awake. Plus I was painting apartments at the other building Mrs. Tokuda owned, down in San Ysidro. Cash, under the table, no strings. It might not sound like much, but at the time I was feeling okay. Generally. There was movement, progression. I couldn't complain, not really. How your life turns out is never what you expect. Driving home at night on the 5, tired and ready for the couch and the balm of cable, I could see the lights of Tijuana in my rearview mirror. I'd half wonder what it would be like to live over there instead of here, the different language, the yearning to be somewhere else, the idea that things could be so much better if it weren't for geography.

It was probably around the sixth or seventh month when I came home after a day of painting (the all-important first coat for an apartment whose occupant, I'd discovered, happened to be a collector of hard-core pornography and rare South American stamps) and found Shell, as usual, marooned on the sofa, preparing the syringe for Hiccup's injection, the cat curled next to her like the docile creature I knew he wasn't. This was Shell's domain. I tried, but I was just too squeamish, and besides, the cat thinks I'm a Nazi so it's hard for him to be calm enough for the shot when I'm the one sticking a needle in him. Shell motioned for me to be quiet. Gently she repositioned Hiccup on his side, steadied the needle like a lifelong junkie, then ushered it into the cat's skin, all in one fluid motion. A pro.

Once that was over, I sat down and gave Shell a kiss that got half lip and half cheek. We went through the how-was-your-day conversation. Hiccup had had enough by then. He wanted to make his statement and publicly scorn my presence, so he ejected himself down to the floor and one-hundred-yard-dashed it toward the hallway.

"I had another one," Shell said.

"Another one," I repeated. "Wow." I had only an hour to eat and shower before I was off to the printers for part two of my day. The mail was in my lap, a big, thick, ridiculous stack. Was it just me or was the amount of mail steadily increasing? Each day it took longer and longer to plow through. More credit card applications, banks I'd never heard of, based in places like Wilmington, Delaware, and Running Brook, Idaho. Jesus, didn't these companies get it? People like us didn't need more plastic, more burdens to fill our days and nights.

"It was just right after lunch," Shell went on, "and I had this flash, a BAM!, you know, in my head, and then I saw a red and white van with lights flashing. So then I do—I don't know—the dishes, whatever, and a little while later I hear this BAM! outside. I look out the bedroom window and there on the street are these two cars, one totally totaled and the other up on the sidewalk all gnarled up like some modern sculpture. They called the ambulance and carried one of the guys away on a stretcher. A car crash. That was the BAM!"

I tossed the mail onto the coffee table next to yesterday's still unopened queries; it was practically the last available space on the table's surface. This was an ongoing issue—the issue of space. Meaning more than just the coffee table. And what with the baby coming and all.

"You know Shell, I've been thinking."

"Uh-oh."

"No, good thinking."

"Oh, good thinking. Well that's okay then. What have you been good thinking about?"

"About your special powers of perception and whatnot."

This was a conversation I'd been trying to have for a while, and now it was happening, more or less unrehearsed. Usually when I had something I wanted to talk to Shell about I'd go over everything in my head, map out the scene, anticipate her comments and reactions. Not this time, though. I was going freestyle. Improvising.

"All right," said Shell, her mouth already souring into a skeptical slant that I knew all too well. She was wearing one of my old T-shirts, something she did a lot of now. The Pretenders: Learning to Crawl Tour '84.

"Well," I started, "what I've been thinking lately is pretty simple actually. Very simple. What it is is this. How can we use this gift? Because that's what it is, a gift. Not for the good of mankind or anything noble like that, but for our own selfish betterment. So I'm thinking: How can we take this gift, harness it so to speak, and then parlay a small investment into something greater? Parlay. Now there's a word I've always wanted to use."

"Rick, what are you getting at?"

"Well if you can see things before they happen then why not take it to the next level? What's that Indian casino Mike and Nancy are always going to?"

"It's up by Temecula, I think. Why?" Her mouth slanted even further. I had my work cut out for me.

"We've got a little money saved up."

"That's baby money."

"We don't need to use all of it. Just some of it. Besides, you're never wrong. You say it yourself all the time. 'I'm never wrong.' It's a gift. Who are we to question the hows and whys of such phenomena?"

"But this is different. This is money we're talking about now, Rick. You know we already have to borrow a shitload from my mom and probably from your sister, too. I don't know about you, but being a mooch doesn't suit me very well. I don't like waking up in the morning and knowing that I owe somebody something. And I'm pregnant, I'm cranky, I'm huge, in case you haven't noticed. It's hard enough for me to go to the market or Target let alone some casino. Some Indian casino."

"Just this one time. We'll go, and if it works, fine, and if not, that's it, it's over. Just once. We won't be greedy. That's where these things usually go wrong. James Caan or whoever gets too greedy, wants too much, won't settle for less. But for us less is already more."

Shell didn't say anything, but I held out hope that she'd come around. Just like me, she can be coaxed into mischief with the right amount of prodding. Of course I'd have to brush up on my gambling. Maybe call Mike for some tips, when to hit, when to stay, what doubling down was all about. Although roulette probably would be best. All you had to do was choose red or black. I wanted to keep it simple, put the least amount of strain on Shell as possible. Red or black. Certainly she could see a color if she could see a car crashing.

"So what are you doing Saturday night?"

"Reading," Shell monotoned, and she pointed to an opened paperback on the coffee table, *Babies for Beginners*, something like that. "And I shouldn't be the only one doing this."

"I know Shell, I know. I promise I'll get up to speed on the baby thing. But this is something we should do. It's just one night. We're in, we're out. It's for the baby after all."

"We'll see," she said.

That night I left the printers early. It must have been three or four in the morning and I'd been up for almost twenty-four hours straight. As I drove I kept dozing off, drifting into the other lane, drifting (in my mind at least) into an alternate existence where I didn't have to work two shifts back to back, didn't have to argue why we shouldn't name our kid Nigel or Percival. I tried everything: slapping my face, rolling down the window, turning up the radio. No matter what I did, though, I couldn't stay awake, my eyelids heavy as pyramids. Somehow I made it home without killing myself or anyone else. I was alive. And for that, I was thankful. I was learning to take small victories wherever I could find them.

We saw the burning blue and pink neon of the Laughing Coyote Casino and Restaurant from the main highway soon after we'd passed through Temecula. There wasn't much else nearby, so it was easy to spot. We lucked out (a sign?) and pulled into the last parking space in the lot and then approached the entrance, over which hung a series of blinking dollar signs and a giant revolving teepee.

"Chee-zee," said Shell, who'd been having some doubts about the whole enterprise on the drive up. She talked nonstop. Her mother would kill her. San Diego radio sucked. Another week of this (the pregnancy, the fat, the waiting) and she'd be totally Sybil. Was this place even legal? Did they use actual American dollars? If the baby knew what we were doing. Maybe the premonitions weren't always right. Etc., etc. But I'd already got the night off from the printers and withdrawn the money. More importantly, I'd managed to convince myself that this was our fate, our destiny.

The air conditioning greeted us with an assaulting, Arctic blast. Inside, the place was packed, swarming with smoke and people and noise. It was pretty much like a regular casino you'd see in Tahoe or Reno, which surprised me. I'd been expecting something lower on the gambling chain, a large asbestos-ridden room decorated in brothel colors and peeling paint, a few tables, a couple of Rat Pack-era slot machines, a handful of lost souls wagering Social Security checks. But it wasn't that at all. The colors were cheery, Southwestern. Families milled about. A fair amount of young people mixed in with the old. Waitresses and dealers wore snappy uniforms. To the far left there was a Denny's-ish restaurant, and next to that a cocktail lounge with free popcorn and a sixties cover band that was slashing and burning its way through a disastrous version of "A Whiter Shade of Pale" as we entered. And yes, the gambling. Rows and rows of blackjack tables. The Wheel of Fortune. Keno. Roulette. Slots. Poker tables way in the back by the bathrooms and cashier stations. And strangely nobody who looked to be Indian.

We started slowly with some video poker. Shell plopped down on the swivel stool and picked the cards as I fed the quarters. After an hour our initial five-dollar investment had netted close to two hundred dollars. Things were moving right along. Next we headed to the restaurant to kill some time before we hit the roulette table. I had a Sitting Bull Burger with cheese, Shell a bowl of Cherokee Three-Bean Chili plus a side of Onondaga Onion Rings. Next door the band wheezed out what I think was supposed to be "Purple Haze." Neither of us spoke much as we ate. Too much tension, too much awareness that the next half hour could be critical—somehow, more and more it seemed like it would either make or break us, and not just financially. Shell finished everything and asked for a dessert menu. I filled out one Keno card after another.

At the roulette table we stood around a while to get the flow of the game and for Shell to practice some. I'd been reading up on roulette. The easiest, simplest bet was to pick a color: red or black. So that was what Shell focused on. Three times she predicted the outcome, and three times she was right. We got our chips.

"Are you ready?" I asked.

"I don't know," she said. "Don't push me. God, I think I have to pee."

"Now?"

"No, it passed. Wait. Aw shit. Let's just do this before I faint or have a heart attack. Or have the kid right here right now."

That was good enough for me. "Make way," I called out as Shell waddled forward and I helped her get situated at the table. "Pregnant woman gambling here." The dealer was paying off from the last game. I was nervous, which usually causes me to say something stupid, and that's exactly what I did. "You don't look like an Indian," I told the guy, thinking I'd make a little small talk, why not. But the dealer shot me this look like he's heard this about a billion times before and if he wasn't in a public place and wearing a uniform and name tag (EARL, it said) he'd strangle me with his belt and leave my body in some snake-infested marsh.

"Place your bets," he ordered, pretty obviously taunting me with his bloodshot eyes. He was short, probably in his forties, and had an Albert Einstein electric shock of hair. You got the sense that he didn't have much of a personal life and that his work wasn't exactly all that fulfilling and that he'd been having a bad day since around the third grade.

People put down their chips, made their bets, just like in the movies and TV. I placed my hands on Shell's shoulders, massaging gently. Scanning the table, I noticed that most of our fellow gamblers looked like extras from *The Andy Griffith Show*. I whispered in my wife's ear:

"Do you see a color?"

"I don't see anything," she said.

"Well maybe if you close your eyes, sweetie."

"I can't believe I'm fucking doing this. Just shut up, all right. Let me think."

Shell took a deep breath. I waited. The dealer waited. Aunt Bee next to us waited. Floyd the Barber across the table, sipping his watery gin and tonic, he waited. Everyone's bet already down. I pinched Shell's shoulders. Hard. Harder.

"Stop it," she snapped.

We needed to make a decision, black or red. Shell was sweating now. I could feel the damp of her skin. We hadn't made love in I don't know how long. Which is a strange thought at such a time, I know, but that's what surfaced in my polluted mind. Black or red. One or the other.

"Does the lady want to make a bet or not?" asked the dealer.

Shell's skin was burning, pure fire. Suddenly my mind slipped elsewhere. There we were on our first date: stupid, boozy, naked, humping away on my couch, our couch. In the morning we ate cereal right from the box and watched cartoons. I didn't know about her asshole dad yet. She didn't know about my less-than-stellar relationship history yet. It seemed so long ago that we'd crossed over into something that neither of us really wanted.

"Red," she said. "Fuck it. Red." And the chips were placed on the felt surface of the table, and the dealer took our bet, all seven hundred—the five hundred we'd agreed on plus the two hundred from video poker—and then there was nothing to do except wait.

For a second I had a flash of doubt. This was wrong. All wrong. This wasn't adult. Soon-to-be parents shouldn't be doing this. I wanted to take the bet back, take Shell home and talk gibberish to her stomach and put on some Mozart. But it was too late. Together we watched the ball sputter and clank all over the spinning wheel. It went on for an eternity, a slow-mo movie moment where the soundtrack swells and your life stops and there's usually a revelation of some kind; in this case, however, the revelation wasn't coming; there was nothing but doubt and panic and an industrial buzzing in my head, and I seriously considered the fact that everything was relative—time, truth, sex, you name it—and that I'd never gotten musicals and probably never would. *Click, click.* Shell had put her hands over her eyes, like a little kid. The ball was immortal. It had a purpose, a power. Finally it began to slow down. Somewhere a baby cried. That was the only sound. That and the ball. Less ferocious now, settling in. *Bounce, click, clack, zlack.* Then it ceased to move as if at last it realized what it wanted, where it desired to be. Number 16. Red. Of course. Otis the Drunk let out a deep moan. The dealer looked pissed. I told Shell to look, that it was all good, that we won. She guessed right. Red. So why was she crying? People were starting to stare. I touched her hair, her wet cheeks. Nothing. "Please," she said. "Just take me home. I just want to be home."

So we doubled our money and walked away. Not a huge deal for some folks, but for us it made a big difference. And as it turned out, we needed it. And as it turned out, we should have been greedy. If the rest of the world is out for blood, then why not us? Truth is, we fucked up.

After that night Shell kept quiet about any more predictions. I could tell, though, that she saw things, bad things. And she was right. The last few months of the pregnancy fizzled away like a faulty Fourth of July sparkler. I ran out of apartments to paint. And not only that: some of the tenants were having problems—vomiting, nausea, shortness of breath—and claiming that unsafe paint had been used. They had hired a lawyer, threatening to sue Mrs. Tokuda, who dropped hints about raising the rent again to cover her legal bills. The printers was cutting back, and pretty soon, as the birth neared, I was officially unemployed and generating zero income. On more than one occasion I found my way back to El Torito. The people were different but they all looked the same as their predecessors: aging, a little haunted by something. I met a woman named Marcia Higbee. She told me I had lips she could trust. Meanwhile Shell's unemployment had run dry. We considered asking my sister for money, again, even though she had her hands full with Nathan and his epilepsy. There was his medicine, the regular doctor visits. The insurance covered some of it, but not everything. Then, a week before Shell's contractions started, just when we were set to bring up the subject of money (as in: can we have some?), Lydia informed us she'd been diagnosed with something called Sick Building Syndrome. The place where she worked, a real estate office in Santee, was contaminated with chemicals. She too experienced vomiting, nausea, shortness of breath. It seemed to be the thing.

What happened was this: the premonitions stopped once the baby was born. Flat out. No more. *Nada mas.* Shell was out of the hospital and back on the couch, nursing our son and circling shows in *TV Guide*, and she said it's over, nothing was there, it had to do with the pregnancy, a temporary situation, and that was that. One of life's little mysteries.

Now it's the three of us. The baby, Tyler's his name (not Nigel, not Percival), is two months old, a mystery of his own. He cries and cries like he's shooting for martyrdom, like a giant mistake has been made. Shell sleeps a lot. Our conversations revolve around two main topics: diapers and bills. The apartment shrinks on a daily basis, filled to the ceiling with baby toys, baby books, baby everything. We had no choice but to fill out some of those credit card applications, first signing up for two, then four. I'm currently putting together a resume and doing sit-ups every night.

And I know it's wrong, I know it's bad and I'm living up to the much-publicized faults of my sex, but I keep wondering how permanent this all is—marriage, wife, now a child. They're part of me yet also separate, removed. There are times when they vanish—*poof, presto,* it's magic—even if we're all in the same room together. And then I'm left with nothing but my lazy random thoughts. Which are never as profound as I'd like. Nothing about mortality or religion or the meaning of existence, or even what it means to live with someone, to share your life like this. Just the everyday clutter that prevents you from getting down to the heart of the matter, or matters. How I drive too fast, stay up too late. How I mumble. How women who are too beautiful seriously frighten me. How there's always the possibility: to disappear, walk away. What else is there to say? Marcia Higbee thinks I'm a software engineer, divorced, trying to put his life back together.

Often at night I stand and watch my son as he sleeps in his crib. He squirms, has difficulty sleeping for more than an hour. I understand. I sympathize as he battles this strange new universe. Always restless. As if he has a troubling knowledge of what's to come. As if he's the one who has the gift now, like it's been passed from mother to son. He sees the future, yes, I'm sure of it, but he won't be able to tell us for a few years. When he finally speaks he'll tell us everything we need to know. But until then we'll just have to live as best we can, and wait.

AMERICA'S FINEST CITY

AMERICA'S FINEST CITY

1.

THE FIRST ABORTION LEFT her numb, feeling dreamy and indistinct, hardly a person at all. When the time came for the second she was beyond that. It was nothing, no big deal. Just another procedure. Why not two? Why not three?

She took the bus to the clinic, both times. Walked the many, many blocks through downtown Oakland. There was no sun and lots of wind. People stared. People knew. The two doctors were different but the same. They didn't say much, just the bare minimum. Men, of course. The nurses were the ones who actually spoke to her.

"Do you have someone to take you home?"

This was the second time, four months ago already, a few years after the first. She had slipped. The time from when she was with Henry. Henry: who didn't handle the news so well. Who kind of disappeared.

"No, I don't," she admitted.

The nurse finished checking her blood pressure. Then she scribbled the results on a chart that hung at the end of her bed.

"How is it?"

"Normal," said the nurse.

No doubt about it: she thought she was doing much better than the first time. Definitely. She knew what to expect, what not to feel and dwell on. The nurse brought over her clothes in a plastic bag.

"You know I'm not supposed to let you leave if you don't have someone," the nurse explained. "You don't have anyone?"

"Okay," she said. "Then there's someone. I lied. There's someone outside waiting for me. They're pulling the car around, right now, as we speak."

The nurse let it go, handed her a piece of paper. The first nurse had done the same. She had been alone then, too.

"Sign here," they both said.

2.

ARLO BOOTH WAS NEW at the hospital. He was there when she got back after her two days off, Monday and Tuesday, replacing Ronnie, one of the night janitors, and Sheila and Mary Jo were all giggly and girly about him, this new guy, Arlo, and she predicted that he would become a topic of conversation and speculation for a good long while. After the bathroom (splashing water on her face, avoiding her blurred reflection in the mirror), she settled in for the shift. Put on her apron. Pulled up her hair. The kitchen smelled like it always smelled: of old food, of leftover things. There were dishes and trays to wash and dry and stack, and then after that the prep for the morning's breakfast. It was Wednesday night, the beginning of her week, when everyone else was already more than halfway through theirs.

The scrubbing started, Sheila to her right, Mary Jo to her left, all at their respective sinks. Suds accumulated. They wore rubber gloves but their hands still turned dry and wrinkled, like old people, and their backs had grown stooped, too, as if prematurely afflicted with the infirmities that should have been awaiting them somewhere in the future. The radio crackled with classic rock, Mary Jo's turn to choose. The three women worked and talked.

"Speak to him yet?" Sheila asked.

"Who?" she said.

"Who? *Who*, she says. You believe this, M.Jo?"

Which made Mary Jo's cheeks brighten and blush, just as it did every time Sheila used the nickname she herself had given her.

"She says *who*," Sheila went on. "Like we get us some fine specimen of man in here every night. You know who."

"Oh, him."

"Yeah, *him*."

"Just got here, you know. There's time. The whole night ahead."

"It's never too soon, never too soon to make the initial approach," said Sheila, who was about as in-your-face as you could get, the opposite of Mary Jo, who was about as not-in-your-face as you could get. "It's never too soon to make an impression." And Sheila added, laughing: "Good or bad."

Changing the subject seemed like a good idea.

"So what happened to Ronnie then?" she asked.

Night people came and went at the hospital, especially the janitors, but Ronnie had been working there since before any of them. He had kids and divorces, a sister with M.S. One time he asked her out on a date. She had to say no. After that, they didn't talk as much.

Mary Jo reached for another stack of food-crusted plates. "Nobody knows," she said.

3.

WORKING NIGHTS WAS A total horror. The disrupted sleep patterns, the empty and late buses, the falling out of touch with friends and family, how the rest of the world was no longer part of your orbit. You were exiled, of the marginalized and sleep-deprived, the heavy-lidded zombies who shuffle endlessly, forget about birthdays and movies and overdue bills, and hardly ever see daylight. Minimum-wage vampires, according to Sheila. But she'd never gotten used to it, the time fuck. Almost a year in and still she felt like a traveler who arrived at her destination without knowing the language, the customs of a strange and terrifying people.

She lived in Hayward and worked in San Francisco. That's where the hospital was, in the Mission District, way out on Cesar Chavez. With the odd hours and the long commute she didn't have much leftover for anything else. When she got home she usually sought refuge on the sofa and sat through the last of the morning shows. Then she'd fall asleep. If she happened to wake, she might drag herself up and crawl into bed. Mostly, though, she'd just stay there sleeping on the sofa, the day developing outside, the TV moving on to the afternoon talk shows, people whose lives were worse than yours.

4.

THE SHIFT CONTINUED, THE night lengthening like a movie that doesn't know when to end. They washed and dried, yawned and commiserated, drank coffee even though they would regret it later. Sheila told a story about how the other day she was standing in line at Wendy's and the person in front of her ordered like ten burgers and the person working there said is that for here or to go and the person in front of her said something like yeah right I'm going sit here and eat all that by myself and the person working there said bitch I don't know your life. Mary Jo confessed that her ex-boyfriend was making overtures. And while her two coworkers talked, she only offered the occasional commentary, laughed or sighed when appropriate.

This was how the nights passed. Stories, advice, counseling. Recounting histories and neglects. Battling pasts and presents. Planning futures. They worked together, spent their breaks together. And only they understood what it was like to be cut off like this: up, awake, working, while everybody else you know slumbers away like children.

The focus tonight, however, kept returning to Arlo. He swept and mopped and cleaned, took out the trash, restocked the cafeteria with paper napkins and Styrofoam cups and the powdered creamer there was never enough of. Whenever he entered the kitchen, he was too shy to come over and introduce himself. But she managed glimpses here and there: he was young, tall, thick-haired. Finally Sheila stepped in.

"Hey Arlo," she called out. "Stop working so hard. You're gonna tire yourself out your first week. Bring yourself over here for a sec. Don't worry. We won't bite. Not yet, anyway."

Arlo smiled, approaching with his mop and bright yellow mop bucket with sloshing brown water. He had sideburns, too, and one of those dimpled chins. Nice.

"Now you already know Ms. Mary Jo, but there's someone else here you haven't had the pleasure of being introduced to, another of our lovely kitchen staff," Sheila said, guiding him toward her like a dance instructor, showing them the proper steps, schooling them on how to move their bodies in unison.

She removed her right glove and they shook hands, like you do when you meet someone new. Hi. *Hi.* Nice to meet you. *Nice to meet you.* Repeat. *Repeat.*

Arlo peeled away, went back to his work, while she resumed her post at the sink, sneaking a last look as he walked away. Sure, he was young, perhaps too young for her or Sheila or Mary Jo, but for the remainder of the night she—and Sheila, and Mary Jo—continued to track him as he performed his duties. He worked hard. Sweated. Moved with a purpose, someone who had plans. You could tell he still cared. Up close, his face was kind, like maybe he knew things.

By the time the shift ended, the sun was up, a declaration in the sky, although she couldn't see any of it. The kitchen was located in the basement, no windows, and so she never came across the hospital's patients much. But she knew they were there, above her, sleeping, breathing, dying; people wounded and damaged, either temporarily or permanently; and they were there every night and every day, just like her.

She said her goodbyes to Sheila and Mary Jo, rode the elevator up, away. Outside, the daylight lashed out at her like a rush of fire. Every morning it was like this. The light a shock, a stab, a fist. And it got in your eyes and skin and teeth, aged you even more. She stood at the bus stop and waited. She'd never met someone named Arlo before.

5.

ON THURSDAY: HER BUS was running late and so she was late for work. On Friday (actually Saturday morning): she got home and there was a message on her machine saying she was qualified to win an exciting vacation at an exciting five-star resort, all she had to do was call back and confirm. On Saturday night, back at the hospital: she kept trying to conveniently run into Arlo but it hadn't worked out. On Sunday: it did. She found him dusting a ceiling light in the hallway just as she came out of the bathroom. He groaned a little as he finished with the light, dragging, his eyes already permanently puffed and his posture lurching like he needed a cane and might fall forward.

"Long night," he said, his voice sounding drained, like an

instrument that's been played too much.

"They always are," she offered back.

"You ever get used to it, being up all night, sleeping in the day?"

"Sort of," she said. "But not really, no."

"That's what I thought," he said. "That's not what they said at the interview though. You get used to it. You adapt."

All right: two coworkers standing around, talking and complaining about work. This was normal, she thought. This was good. This was a start.

6.

"CHANGE THE LOCKS," SHEILA said. "Change your phone number. Get some mace. Protect yourself."

This was directed at Mary Jo. Yesterday she arrived home and found her ex-boyfriend sprawled out on the couch, like he still lived there, like he was king.

"He's just bitter is all," Mary Jo tried to explain.

"I know," said Sheila. "That's why. That's why you need to protect yourself."

They were on their break in the cafeteria, sharing a cigarette, passing it around like a joint. You weren't supposed to smoke in there but nobody was around so nobody cared.

"Now with someone like our Mr. Arlo, see, it's different," Sheila continued. "That's what I've been trying to say. He's young. He's fresh. You don't want no baggage."

The cigarette, almost down to the butt, went around again, from her to Sheila to Mary Jo. The break was now technically over, but they were lingering.

"What about you, Miss Lovely?" Sheila asked her. "How about your turn for a change? Have any men stories you'd like to put on the table tonight?"

"Sure, I've got my stories," she said.

"Then let's hear one. Looking like you look, I bet you got some good ones."

There were things she told Sheila and Mary Jo, and things she didn't. She was closer to them than she was to anybody. Still, she couldn't give like they gave. She hadn't told them about the clinic, about Henry, about any of it.

"One time a guy I was dating, he slashed my tires," she said, hoping she wouldn't have to say more than that.

"That's good," said Sheila. "Slashed tires are good."

"What happened to him?" Mary Jo asked.

"He inherited some money. Moved to Phoenix, last I heard. We better get back."

"We got time," said Sheila. "The dishes aren't going anywhere. Let's hear another one. With more details this time. Take it slow. Give it a beginning and middle and end. Make it a story."

"I don't think so," she said, standing. "That's my one. That's my one for tonight."

7.

HER TWO DAYS OFF: it was mostly sleep and recovery, sleep and recovery, getting her body rested and ready for the upside-down week ahead.

8.

SHE RECONSIDERED THE SAD men that had previously paraded through her life. Not specific names. But the type. The type of man she typically ended up with. By nature they were distant and often angry about things, matters they couldn't control. Simmering men. Hurtful men. Men who for whatever reason wanted to take you down with them, keep you down. For many years it hadn't mattered to her. She went along for the ride. They did offer their comforts, routines. And when the time came, they were easy to shed. If you never expected too much, then you never got too disappointed. That was the theory at least.

But Arlo—Arlo stood out, shined brighter, gave her a vague, humming hope even though it wasn't based on anything solid, not yet. They had hardly spoken after all, just passing pleasantries, and as the next few shifts at work finished, nothing had progressed all that much. But maybe that was better. Better than the other way, how it usually went, too fast too soon, because she could imagine and wonder and not be messed up by what already had happened. And so he regularly popped into her head, no matter where she was, no matter the time of day. Dreams, too. Arlo smiling. Arlo sweeping. Arlo unbuttoning the top buttons of his nametagged shirt…

And more than once she pictured going home with him after work, the two of them tired but not that tired, horny as teenagers, rolling on the floor, half naked, mildly pornographic, hungry for something, something to transform them, to take them away from the reality of who they were and who they weren't. She let him know with her eyes whenever she had the chance: it was possible.

9.

BACK HOME FROM WORK—and there was Henry, surprise, camped out on her doorstep, sitting on the floor and blocking her entrance, drunk, with his shoes off. A friend of his used to live in her building. There had been a party. There had been margaritas. That was how it began.

"What're you doing here?" she asked.

Henry: who'd been a band-aid, a way to cover one of her lonely parts. But it didn't hold. Temporary, the clock ticking from the moment they were introduced, maybe even before that, and she probably had led him to believe it was more than it was, which wasn't the first time. And so she deserved some of the blame. Some but not all. And she had slipped.

"Waiting for you," he answered, smiling like he'd said something very clever. The alcohol and cigarettes so strong it was like you could practically see the fumes escaping from his hunched body. "Just happened to be in the neighborhood and all. Just a friendly ex-boyfriend visit."

It had ended with Henry freaking after she told him she was pregnant. She had been planning on breaking it off anyway, but he had made it easier for her, in a way. And now she could be righteous. She could be pissed off and dramatic. She had the right.

"Long time no see," she said.

Henry squinted up at her, doing his best to focus his boozed eyes. "You're skinny."

A curtain was closing over his face, the information sinking in, seeping through the liquor.

"Why thank you," she said, trying to take it in a different direction, watching him curl his knuckles and then hearing them shift and crack. "And you're drunk. And your shoes are off. And you're sitting in front of my door."

"You shouldn't be skinny."

She sifted through her purse for her keys. Meanwhile Henry attempted to stand, faltering, once, twice, then succeeding. He was tall, though not as tall as Arlo, and heavy, the hulking frame of an athlete in decline. He worked construction. All of his friends worked construction as well. Only they never seemed to do much work, much constructing. Just hung out and complained, arguing about the Raiders or the A's or how so-and-so's wife had so-and-so by the balls and he didn't even know it.

"What'd you go and do?"

"Oh I get it. I don't see you in how long and then you show up and start acting like you're still in the picture. Like you got rights. Why the sudden interest now? Because at the time, at the time you sure weren't interested. I believe your exact words were *I don't want no part of this, count me out.*"

Turning away, Henry stalked down the hallway and back, running his hands through his hair several times. It was eight a.m. or thereabouts, the morning outside gushingly bright and alive, and all the regular people with regular jobs and regular lives were having coffee or just waking up or hitting the snooze button and thinking *five more minutes.* And here she was with Henry, who just now picked up one of his shoes and launched it down the hall. Then he picked up the other one and did the same. Throwing them with great force, but both shoes landing limply, hardly making a sound. Time to get inside.

She had her key out, ready. But he was blocking the door again, and apparently he wasn't moving out of the way. Better say something. Remembering rule number one when dealing with a drunk person:

don't tell them they're drunk. And she'd already done that once. So she didn't do it a second time. Even though she wanted to spit that at him: *You're drunk.* So something else:

"Why'd you come here in the first place?"

At first Henry didn't answer, just stood there, brow lowered and head cocked in masculine disbelief, like a guy in a police lineup, guilty now, guilty forever.

Then he said, "Doesn't matter why I came. What matters is what you did."

It was all about maneuvering now, like a game of chess, but with words, too.

"Look," she told him, "I just worked my eight hours plus the bus. I'm about to pass out I'm so tired. We are not having this conversation now. I'm going to open the door. You're going to step aside. And I'm going inside my apartment and sleep."

"You what—think you can play Jedi mind games on me or something?"

He made himself laugh, he tilted forward, and this provided her with an opportunity. Quickly she managed to drive the key into the lock and squeeze inside the apartment. There was, however, a bit of a struggle before she could close the door. He knocked and pounded and kicked, splintering some of the door's cheap renter's wood. Then he gave up. Down the hallway she heard him yelling, "Bitch. Bitch. You shouldn't let that bitch live in your building."

10.

IN FACT SHE DID have a child, a son, Marcus, who lived with a religious aunt in Tennessee. It was better that way. At Christmas and on his birthday she sent him a present, just a little something, she couldn't afford much but she tried, signing the card, *Love, Mom.* For years she'd written the "o" in Mom as a heart. But last year she decided it was time to stop, her son was almost ten and probably embarrassed by touches like that.

And now every time she visited or he visited (once, maybe twice a year) it was like meeting a brand-new person. He had different tastes, liked different music and TV shows and cartoon characters. She used to recognize parts of her in him, both physically (his eyes, the unfortunate underbite) and otherwise (his sense of humor, how he liked his cereal soggy). But she had faded from him. There was no part of her left in Marcus, her son, except her blood and genes and DNA, all the things that are there but you can't see.

11.

As always she took her bus across the Bay Bridge, her daily commute, her daily penance, from Hayward to San Francisco, getting off downtown at the Transbay Terminal and then having to catch another bus to the hospital, practically a two-hour ordeal each way. The only consolation of the trip was the sight of the city sparkling at night, all lit up like a magical land from a children's book. She stared at the tall buildings, so wise and glittering, and wondered what it would be like to work in such a place, with normal hours, with a garage to park your car in, to sit at a desk, to have a computer, to go home in rush-hour traffic, someone there when you pulled up in the driveway, to even *have* a driveway.

Arlo called in sick that night. She missed his sweeping and trips into the kitchen. How he smiled then looked down quick-like when he first saw her. She liked that. When had she ever known a man who was shy? She thought of him often during her shift. So did Sheila and Mary Jo.

"That boy is sweet," said Sheila.

"Sweeter than sweet," cooed Mary Jo.

She didn't say anything. It was best to hold back sometimes. Sometimes if you said something out loud it wouldn't come true.

12.

The phone rang and she let the machine answer. Whoever it was didn't leave a message. She rolled over on the couch, tried to fall back asleep. Her neck ached, her fingers throbbed. How old do you have to be in order to get arthritis?

At some point the phone rang again. People were out there, in the world, and there was nothing you could do about it.

13.

No, she hadn't settled on some big life decision. She had been thinking, sure, realizing that there were patterns and certain behaviors. There was a time when there had been too many men, too much sharing of herself for all the wrong reasons. But the job at the hospital had taken care of that. Had made her untouchable, apart. (Henry being the only one to sort of break through, and look what happened with that.) So maybe, then, it had all been for the best. Her employment situation yielded some perspective, a new way to see herself. Before, she had believed in luck. There was good luck and bad. How you lived with the consequences of that fundamental fact was the real concern. But maybe, she was now willing to consider, maybe there was more to it than luck. Maybe it didn't have to be one way or the other. Maybe you could stop, change direction. Maybe you could surprise yourself.

Arlo was back the next night. He still looked somewhat under the weather—weak and feverish. His breaks lasted longer, he wiped sweat from his brow with his sleeve and kept staring at the kitchen's clock whenever he came in to do something. He said even less than usual. And when he did say something, his voice was cloudy and deep from being sick.

"Mmmmm, sexy," whispered Sheila.

That turned out to be the night, or morning, at the end of their shift, that she and Arlo got to really talking. It was in the parking lot. And it was just one of those times when things fall into place without much effort. You're not even trying. It just happens. Naturally. Small talk but nice talk. Not like when it's all forced and obvious and stupid, when both people know it's a game and where it's all heading.

"You sure you're feeling okay?" she wanted to know.

"I'll be all right. Thanks," he said. "I just can't afford to be missing too much work. I need the money."

"Don't we all."

He couldn't look her in the eye for very long. The parking lot was filling up fast; cars, day people passing by. He'd look at her then glance away. Look; then glance away. That was good, she thought.

"How long was it you say you been working here?" Arlo asked.

"Too long. A year."

"And before that, what?"

"Anything and everything. Cleaning houses, temping. I worked with kids. Little ones. My cousin, she had a family daycare for a while. I helped with that."

She found herself zeroing in on his neck, the strength of it, the smooth grace. Had she ever noticed this before, fully, his beautiful neck? That was the thing about Arlo. He always surprised you. He always seemed to offer something new every time you saw him or thought about him. Like there were layers. And today it was his neck. And it looked like something to lick, to taste. Her tongue coiled inside her mouth, wanting, waiting.

"A year," he said, hands in his pockets now. "That can be a long time."

"Tell me about it."

And the other thing with Arlo, what repeatedly struck her, and what made him different, or seem different, was how he didn't have this fucked-up idea of how he was supposed to act, how he was supposed to be, and then he'd try to live up to that no matter what. He was just himself. And that appeared to be enough for him. With Arlo, she thought, or someone like Arlo, she could finally be with a man who raised you up instead of pulled you down.

"A year ago—let's see. A year ago," he said, "and I was still living in San Diego."

"San Diego," she said, tucking her hair behind her left ear, only to have it quickly spill free again. A horn blared and echoed through the parking lot. "I had a friend who lived there. Used to live there."

"America's finest city," said Arlo. "San Diego. That's what they say."

There was a pause. She thought of what it would be like to probe that dimple with the tip of her tongue. Then they started talking again. As often as she dared, she released that smile, that look that said *yes*. What more could she do?

14.

ARLO HAD A CAR. Once they were on the Bay Bridge, she peered back at San Francisco, behind and to her left, the sun fresh and new in the sky, Arlo's profile shadowed and noble-seeming, like a president on a coin. She looked and then looked away. Back in the parking lot felt like yesterday, last week. There was a song on the radio that she could never remember the name of. Whatever it was called, it was like smoke inside her, potent and rising.

Her apartment smelled of cat and flowers left out too long. She did the brief tour, offered the usual excuses about the place being a mess, not expecting anyone, there was never enough time for cleaning and laundry and shopping, etc. Arlo trailed her, nodding like an inspector of some kind. When he asked about the cracks in the front door she told him it was from a long time ago.

They ended up in the hallway, just standing there. He seemed a little unsure of what next, so she touched his shoulder, then his neck (that neck!), then lips; they were soft, the lips of someone in a dream.

When they were ready, they drifted toward her bedroom and the bed.

"I just want to make sure," he said. "Are you…Are you taken care of? Or do you want me to—"

"Don't worry, Arlo," she stopped him. "It's taken care of. I learned. Thanks for asking though."

And she helped him in, and he started to go too fast, she had to tell him to slow down, and he did, they went slow, slower, backtracking, and she pulled him closer, as close as they could get, so that there was less distance in the world, a greater opening somehow. His skin felt like skin: beautiful, warm.

15.

THE KITCHEN SEEMED LIKE the right place to be. There was a small, round table in the corner with chairs that didn't match. The refrigerator was old and made an intermittent ticking noise and resembled the refrigerator from *I Love Lucy*.

"Hungry?" she asked.

"Yeah, sure."

"Eggs okay?"

"Sure. Eggs are fine. Eggs are great."

He was watching her now, a woman in her kitchen, familiar with everything, removing stuff from the fridge, firing up the coffee, and she could sense the curious casting of his eyes. She liked it, the feeling of him watching her. Not judgmental or anything. Just watching. Just curious.

"I hope I don't get you sick," he said. "With my cold I mean."

"You won't. I can tell."

He told her that the job at the hospital was just temporary, a way to get through school. He had one more year to go and then he'd see.

"College, right?" she joked.

"Yeah, college, I'm not that young."

She asked what he studied and when he said the natural sciences she left it at that.

Sunlight streamed into the kitchen, thick as paint. Arlo sat in a patch of brimming yellow, sunning himself like a cat would. And just then her gray tabby lounged into the kitchen and stood as if waiting for instruction.

"That's Norman," she said. "He doesn't come out much anymore. You should be honored."

"Norman. That's a good name for a cat," he said.

She cooked up the eggs, adding some salsa from a jar. It was nice to listen to the sounds of food being prepared: the utensils, the spatula working the skillet, drawers opening and closing.

"My breakfast specialty: salsa eggs," she said, serving him a plateful of scrambled eggs flecked with tomato and onion along with toast.

"Thanks, wow."

But he didn't dive in. He was going to wait for her.

"This is out of the blue," he began.

"That's okay."

"But do you know what an egret is?"

"A what? No, I don't think so."

She filled her own plate, grabbed the salt and pepper if need be. The coffee was just about ready.

"They're these birds," he went on. "They're white. And tall. And skinny. And they have these really really long necks. I don't know. Anytime I see them they make me happy. They make me smile." Arlo paused. He still hadn't started eating yet. "I don't know why I thought of that. Maybe because I used to see them in San Diego by the lagoons right off the 5, and we were talking about San Diego earlier, back at work. Or maybe I'm happy."

She kissed him from behind when he said that, and sat at the table, too.

Then they got down to the serious business of grubbing. She followed his chewing and swallowing and wiping of his mouth with the paper towel she'd given him as a napkin. She cautioned herself not to get too far ahead with this. After all, the rest of the day would come, eventually, and why would anyone think otherwise, and they would need to sleep at some point and then later talk about what had happened and whether this was going to turn into something regular or not. But for now they sat there eating and bathing in the brewing light, saying nothing, wondering who would be the first to speak.

ARE YOU OKAY?

ARE YOU OKAY?

NAKED IS NOT GOOD. Naked is not sexy. Naked is not, suddenly, tragically, what you want to be.

But: here you are anyway, naked. Totally. Completely. Shockingly. Nude. As nude as nude can be, and how the word itself, *nude*, sounds-feels-tastes exactly like it should. Never have you been so nude, so naked, so fundamentally revealed. You wonder: is it the light? No, it is not the light. The light in the room (hers) is minimalist and warm. It's actually a calming, campfire-y glow. So no: it's you all right. It's your nakedness. The fact of this. The lapsed biology of this. It's something— something is pulling you away from the slutty awe and allure of the moment, and this is not good either. This is, in fact, bad.

Eye contact—when was the last time there was confirmed I-see-you you-see-me eye contact? Minutes ago. Not since the removal of your socks, her panties, both of you busying yourselves with the grave mechanics of undressing. All distractions, all utilitarian preparations gone now. The daiquiris starting to wear off, too. You're afraid to look; she's afraid to look. *Several* minutes ago, and counting. Somehow (instinct?) you both paddle over to your respective sides of the bed, which is fluffy and white and suggestive of cumulus. Moving is like moving upstream, like swimming underwater against a mighty current. You are salmon people: pink, vulnerable. The question then becomes: under the comforter or on top? Yet another impasse. How many can one encounter withstand?

Though to be fair, it's her nakedness as well. This is also disturbing. Because you are both older, beyond the push of forty, both well versed in the body's betrayals and declines. This is not magazines. This is not movies. This is a small bedroom in a large apartment complex where in the background you can hear the nocturnal comings and goings of neighbors, bass-heavy stereos, cats wanting to be let inside. She has had children. One breast seems lower, bigger than the other. The skin sags and hangs where you'd expect, the sporadic blemishes draw the eye like glints of glass. But there is a truth and a bluntness to her shape. You aren't complaining. It's not that. And you are not not attracted to her. It's just that it makes you a little sad, is all.

You think back to the bar. Remarkably it's been only what—a half hour since you departed in agreement: her place, because the kids weren't there and it was closer and there was no way your apartment would do. Swaggering out into the night like a couple of professional club-goers. It was a bar adjoined to a Hollywood-themed chain restaurant, and both bar and restaurant were empty of customers but crowdedly decorated with the memorabilia of lesser celebrities who, you thought, didn't really deserve their own memorabilia. (Stephen Baldwin's money clip? Ally Sheedy's cigarette case?) You talked about music. You talked about the coming fall TV season. You talked about when you love someone and it's like a part of you disappears but you don't mind. You ran a tab because why not, it's Friday night, and because it's not like she's an anonymous pickup. She's a coworker with whom you've bonded during the past few months, finding each other amid the hundreds of scuttling employees who call BriteTech home. Divorced, single parents, aging, unsatisfied at work, similarly wounded by the world—there was plenty to commiserate about. And commiserate you did. Lunches, breaks, after-work drinks, occasional carpooling. Plus a balanced, enthusiastic exchange of emails, voicemails, and instant messages. The intimacy increasing day by day, week by week, until the narrative arc of the relationship had reached its turning point. Today, tonight. Too many drinks. Too many whispery revelations at one sitting. A hand brushed a thigh. A glance was returned, affirmed. Marvin Gaye's "Sexual Healing" seeped out of the sound system.

Now, however, there is no soundtrack. Only two bodies, one storyline. You've arrived at your desired destination—well, desired is perhaps too strong a word. You've thought about it. Wondered about it.

What would it be like if. And now it's here. Live. In real time. You've both laid the foundation for what is about to happen/not happen. And you are still standing there at the bed. You are still naked. Your penis curves a bit to the left, her right. You are either half erect or half limp.

To be clothed, at home, driving, navigating a wiggly shopping cart while spending way too much time deliberating over what you should buy: they are all better options than this, than being naked. You can't even enjoy the essentials anymore. Sex, sports, food—when was the last time food was anything more than fuel? You've lost the ability to relax, to "chill," as your son would put it, he of the weekly phone call, which has become a duty, a penance for you both, but it's all you have, so you hit the speed dial button every Sunday evening at approximately the same time, the conversations growing shorter and shorter, devolving into a clipped Q&A format, you like a probing journalist, and he like an interview subject who doesn't want to disclose too much. Looking back—and why not look back when you're nude in front of a coworker, collapsing sexually, with your budding belly catching the faintest hint of stale air conditioning—there have been failures, sure. Not as grand as some, but certainly worse than others. A connect-the-dots trail of fuckups and stutters and regrets. This is not the life you envisioned, ever. Somewhere your son is sleeping in a room you've never been in, never seen, in another state, in another time zone. He is twelve and moody. And somewhere your wife sleeps next to a new and improved husband: taller, sturdier than you, financially more secure, more vigorous, more ambitious, more everything. He has a goatee and listens to smooth jazz. He works out three times a week, minimum. You remain skeptical about the timing of everything. Your wife says she met him after, after she knew it was over. It had nothing to do with Clay. You say no. She, your wife, has always been hazy on the chronology of the whole thing, perhaps wanting to spare you the pain, perhaps wanting to bequeath you a lifetime's supply of uncertainty and tunneling doubt. You thought your marriage was fine, rock-solid. Sadly, you still think of your marriage as fine, rock-solid, even though the divorce papers were signed more than three years ago. And counting. How could two people who shared so much and were so close be so far away from each other, then and now? You'd really like to know.

Does my face, my body betray all this? you wonder. Sure. Probably. Most likely. Though she—Barb, not your wife, the naked woman's name is Barb Sobol, she works as an assistant to the director of human resources and lives in Burbank and was born in Minnesota and is lactose intolerant but once a week likes to treat herself to a grande Mocha Coconut Frappucino in spite of the repercussions afterward—doesn't seem to display any recognition of this. She pulls the comforter and sheets back. And that is that. Underneath it is.

But before she retreats into bed, she pauses. This you notice out of the corner of your eye. How should you proceed? Do you start mumbling excuses or carry on as though everything was fine and hope for the best? Then it happens: eye contact. However, you fail to hold her gaze for very long; it's quick, brief, a camera flash of time that dazes you, makes you blink. You look away. Look away and note the framed photographs on the dresser. Vacations. Lakes. Wet hair and uncomplicated smiles. But this is evidence you'd rather not confront. So you concentrate on the open closet that's behind her, that's overflowing with clothes and boxes and shoes, as if it's inadequate, not enough to contain what needs to be contained.

Wait. Barb has said something. You realize this belatedly, after the fact. She's waiting for a response.

"Sorry?" you ask.

"Are you okay?" she says.

And it is not until you hear this sound, her voice, Barb Sobol's voice, concerned and maternal, that you fully concede to yourself that no, you are not okay. You have been crying. For some time, apparently. Here, on the cusp, on the verge of sex, fucking, intercourse, coitus, relations, whatever, the first real opportunity for such contact since you don't want to say when—with your wife, that's when, with the woman who still circulates in your blood and probably will forever, and how you long for the time, only moments ago, when you could be classified as half erect—and you are crying. Maybe it will pass. Maybe you'll be able to follow through despite all this pregame activity. You can still perhaps redeem yourself here.

But the heaving keeps coming, it's a vibrant, sucking rush, and everything's blurred and wet and you're out of breath and you don't know when it will subside, soon, you hope, soon, but it might take a while, and this is what you want to tell Barb, sweet, sweet slightly gap-toothed Barb, who deserves better (don't we all), just to give her a general heads up about what's going on, to reassure, to let her know that it's not her fault and she deserves better, only you can't talk right now because of the heaving, the continuing influx of added air, but you will be able to, talk that is, at some point, soon perhaps, the words will rise eventually, and that's what you'd say if you could.

RENTERS

RENTERS

THE DREAM WAS ABOUT horses. I was riding one. Or at least I think I was riding one. Because really, what I remembered most later, right after waking up, during that fuzzy but somehow also kind of clear spell of time when dreams are still picture-fresh and haven't started to run away from you yet—what I remembered most about the dream was this feeling of movement. There was the wind pressing against my face, the soft coolness of that. And my body bouncing up and down. And closing my eyes. And then with the wind again as I seemed to go faster and feel lighter, all without having to hold on to anything. And then, finally, forgetting my name and who I was and all the things that were piling up and not going away. But it all stops abruptly, a rope pulls me back, back, because my brother, Ryan, has apparently hit me. Hard. Twice.

"Get the fuck up," he says, pounding my shoulder a third time just because.

Ryan is older, fourteen as of last month, when he announced that he would be spending his birthday with his new high-school friends and not his family. Recently, too, he decided that cursing makes him cool. And who knows. Maybe it does. I wouldn't be the person to ask.

Still cloudy-headed, still pasty-mouthed, I mutter something back to my brother. Not words, really, more like caveman grunts. The idea behind the sounds, though, is *hey, what gives, what's going on?* Ryan understands. More and more we don't even have to speak to communicate. It's mostly our faces and our eyes and the way we nod or point. And that's usually enough. He's my brother, and I know him better than I know myself. We share a room, a bathroom. And, of course, our parents. We know things that no one else knows.

But there's one last thought before Ryan rips off the blankets and calls me a dork-wad and I have to admit defeat: can you close your eyes in a dream, can you fall asleep in a dream, can you know that you're both sleeping in your bed and also sleeping in your head?

"Dad," Ryan tells me. And that's all he has to say.

It's strange being awake this early. The alarm won't go off for another hour at least, and the world outside is dark and quiet and unknown. People sleeping or maybe rolling over, taking showers, spraying on deodorant, zipping zippers, doing whatever it is they do in the morning. Except, I guess, people who live in different time zones. To them it's later in the morning or afternoon or even at night, their day might even be over, those people across the oceans in places you see on maps and globes but who still somehow don't seem real.

I start getting dressed, my clothes cold from the night before, which I hate, which means I'll never be warm all day. It's Tuesday. Tomorrow is Wednesday. I listen but there's nothing. Which is weird. The silence. No TV, no dishes, no doors. And no Ryan complaining about this or that, or me being told that I pay attention too much. It's rare, the quiet now, like finding a quarter in your pocket that you forgot about, and if it wasn't for my brother digging like a dog for a pair of clean socks I'd be able to almost enjoy it.

Secrets are hard to keep in our house because you can hear everything from everywhere. And that's because it's mostly empty and there's not much furniture, and so sounds echo through the rooms and down the halls and up the stairs. We're renters, is the thing. We don't own the house, it's not actually ours, and everyone in the neighborhood seems to know this. Because our lawn is brown. Because we don't have a barbecue in the backyard. Because the leaves never get raked. People walk by with their dogs on leashes and their babies in strollers and instead of saying hello they smile without showing their teeth.

But I remember the first day we moved in, six months ago, and how it was this big deal, moving from an apartment where not all the windows opened to a house—a house!—where you had to walk outside to get the mail. Even though we couldn't afford to buy what the house needed, what would make it more of a home, we'd go from room to room, excited by all the space, the possibilities there. My parents talked more, watched movies together. Ryan and I tried harder, too.

It didn't take long, though, before our new life felt like our old life, with just a different place where we slept. Once we were sort of settled in, the neighbor ladies with the hair and nails brought us casseroles and cold cut platters. They looked around: Where was the cushiony sofa? The dining room table and matching chairs like so? The glass cabinet with snow globes and sports trophies? The framed pictures of kids who get straight A's and make their beds without being told to? We had none of that stuff, just the basics, what you could pack in a rented U-Haul trailer, our dad's truck, and our mom's Nissan Sentra. They looked and looked and looked but didn't find what they were looking for. They asked what kind of mortgage we had. My parents were melting, their bright future slipping through their fingers like sand. Ryan burped. The ladies didn't come back.

Just as I finish tying my shoes (they're tight, I'll need another pair soon but I haven't said anything yet), Ryan buzzes past me and says, "Move it ass-dick, let's go."

And so we barrel down the stairs like firemen who just got a call. I ask Ryan for details about what's happening and he says shut up and mind your own beeswax jizz-head and I say come on and he says all right: "Dad shows up and I'm like dead asleep and he wakes me up, he keeps shaking me until my eyes open and I'm like what? He's got the breath, and but he tells me to wake you up too and to then meet him in the truck in the garage, pronto, in five minutes, which was like five minutes ago already. There. Satisfied, Sherlock Holmes?"

From the kitchen we can hear the tired rumble of the truck's engine. And then there's nothing to do except go into the garage and there's our father in the front seat, waiting. We squeeze in, squeeze together, the three of us, and try not to look at him but we do anyway. His eyes are red and puffy, and his mouth is open like he's just heard something he can't bring himself to believe. He hasn't shaved. His whiskers seem sharp, sharpened, like they could cut your fingers if you touched them. Basically he looks like he's been up all night. Which he has, I guess.

I notice the car doesn't have much gas, maybe an eighth of a tank. I don't say anything, but I'm worried. I don't know where he's taking us. Or why.

For just a moment, a blink-and-you-forget-it-before-you-even-know-it one, as we're backing out of the driveway and onto the street that's our street, technically, but has never really felt like our street, I think that maybe he's kidnapping us. But since nowadays he usually doesn't want much to do with us, why, I wonder, would he go to all the trouble and risk of going to jail and winding up on *America's Most Wanted*? It doesn't make sense.

He stops the truck. We're not moving. Ryan and I look at each other, then at the house, out there in the dark and cold, no lights on, with our mother sleeping inside.

He says, "You guys have never seen where I work, have you?"

We both shake our heads: no.

The walls are thin. I walk in on conversations. My mom calls her sister practically every night. I don't sleep well. Plus how sound travels, the echo effect. This all means, then, that I know more than I probably should. Ryan doesn't listen as much as I do. Especially now that he's older, wants a guitar, has touched girls behind the Circle K on Lincoln Boulevard.

"What's the point?" he likes to say. "What's gonna happen is gonna happen either way, the folks are the folks, and I'll be outta here when I'm outta here, so what the fuck?"

And I guess he's right.

First, side streets. Then the freeway, where there are only a few other cars, all with their headlights on, two white beams pulling them forward against their will. I watch them as they pass or we pass. The people inside hold their giant lidded cups of coffee and take long slow sips like they were drinking a secret potion that makes them live forever, or at least longer. Their hair is still wet from the shower and they check themselves in the rearview mirror. They sip and stare. I imagine they all have their radios going. The news. Traffic. Weather. Sports. The voices of men and women who tell you about the world.

As he drives my father has a toothpick in his mouth. This is normal. More often than not there's a toothpick between his lips. Now he scrapes his teeth with it while his other hand rests on the bottom part of the steering wheel, the way he always drives, like he's barely controlling the car. When he's done working his teeth, he sucks on the wood, switches it from one side of his mouth to another, as if he can't decide which is the better place. Then, sticking with the right side, he dangles it there. It's so familiar that without a toothpick his face seems wrong. When I picture him it's always with the toothpick, a small pointy weapon that's part of his mouth, a warning.

My mom hates the toothpicks. She tells him use some floss, it's gross. He tells her he likes the old-fashioned things, if it was good enough for his father, then it's good enough for him. And every time she finds a soggy toothpick on a table or counter or even the floor, she holds it up, like evidence, as if saying "See?" and then throws it in the trash.

He changes lanes, then changes back when the car in front of us is going too slow.

"Aren't you guys excited?" he says. "You should be excited. But you don't look excited. Don't you want to know what your father does for work, where he goes every day?"

We did. We definitely did. We only knew that our father worked in an office and wore a collared shirt and a tie and slacks and his blue windbreaker, and pretty much everybody there was stupid except for him and this one other guy, Donald, who came over to the house once and broke a lamp. But we were silent. We were stone. We were TV sets without the sound on.

"Come on," he keeps going. "This'll be fun. I know it's early but Christ. Perk up already. Show some enthusiasm for your old man. We're the men here. Just the men. This is what I do every day. Make this drive. Look out at this road, these streets. Count down the minutes until I get there. Ten. Nine. Eight. How many miles are left. Getting closer and closer. And I'm not doing this for my health, you know. If it was up to me…God, you guys are thick. What am I going to do with you?"

He looks over his shoulder and changes lanes again.

Ryan is a way better name than Steven. I've given it plenty of thought over the years, and I'd take Ryan over Steven any day. But that's not the way it worked out. I'm Steven. Ryan is Ryan. That is something that isn't going to change. Even if, when I get older, and I do all the legal stuff you have to do to officially change your name, I'd still know, deep down, underneath the new car shine of Keith, of Kyle, of Tyler: I'm Steven.

And Ryan would always be older, too.

Now there's Tony Pennisi. Now there's Rory Hines. And Charlene Moorehouse, with her tight shirts that show off her navel ring. They call. They come by. They leave and go places. Ryan is home less and less, and I want to be gone, away, too. Instead I stay in our room, reading the books I check out from the library, finishing one and then picking up another, thinking of what I'd be doing if Ryan were there.

Ryan says there's a lot I don't understand, that I'm still just a kid. His world is getting bigger. And mine, it seems, is getting smaller.

We reach the right freeway exit and now there's some light in the sky, cracks of color here and there. Every now and then I look at the gas gauge and worry. We go on one of those streets that seem to repeat itself every few blocks: gas stations, Home Depots, Taco Bells, Burger Kings. After that some apartments or a storage place or a used car lot, and then the same scene all over again.

"I'm hungry," I announce. It's one of those things where I hadn't planned on saying anything, it just came out on its own.

"It's barely even light yet," my dad says, and then makes a fist with his right hand and blows into it several times; the heater in the truck only half works. When he's done, he goes on: "Who gets hungry this early? Usually you'd be asleep right now. How can you possibly be hungry?"

"Well I am is all," is what I say.

Right then we happen to be passing a McDonald's, big surprise. I can tell he's in one of those moods where he's too tired or too distracted to argue. So he turns into the drive-thru. The voice from the speaker where you order is all *wah-wah-wah* like the teachers in Charlie Brown.

Me, I get two Sausage McMuffins with egg. Ryan orders pancakes and orange juice. My dad: coffee plus a hash brown.

"Don't eat yet," he instructs us. "It's not much farther. Just wait."

So we wait, the bags of food on our laps. The bags are warm. We can smell what's inside. Suddenly, though, I'm not so hungry anymore. It's another one of those things: You think you want something, then you get it, then you don't want it anymore. It loses something between the wanting and the having.

"I feel like I'm always failing you somehow," he said one time.

They have these conversations that are really the same conversation over and over, with different words but the same meaning.

I'll be in my room reading, listening.

"Please don't tell me that," she said back. "Please. I don't want to hear it. I don't want to know."

The parking lot is empty. In front of us is the place where my dad works. It's one of those buildings where the windows are black on the outside so you can't see inside. Next to it are two other buildings exactly the same. There's grass and plants and trees and flowers. Everything wet from the night before. The asphalt, too.

Like I said before, we know our father works in an office, and that he also complains about having to be there all the time. Other than that it's up to our imagination. Work was just a place he went, like we went to school, you didn't have a choice about it. When he comes home and plops down on the couch or drags himself upstairs, we all know to let him be, to let him settle in before we say anything. Sometimes it's five minutes. Sometimes it's longer.

Still, I'm curious. About what he does all day, what he says to other people and what they say to him. In movies and TV shows I keep an eye out for anyone who acts like him and dresses like him so I might discover some clues.

"They forgot the fucking syrup," Ryan announces. And Dad just shoots him this look like: That's my territory, don't even think about it, bub. Ryan gets quiet, eats, licks his fingers like he's in a commercial.

It's silent then as we sit and eat in the truck. The smell of the food is heavy: the sausage, the egg, the pancakes, the grease. It's hard to think of anything else but the smell. My dad isn't drinking the coffee because it's too hot. He takes off the lid and the steam rises up and mixes in with his breath, which I can see. It's that cold.

And then my dad says, "I wanted you guys to see this. It seemed important a few hours ago, earlier, back at the house. For some reason. For some reason it seemed important. I had something I wanted to tell you, too. But now. Now I don't know. It's just a building. It doesn't mean anything..."

And his voice trails off, drifts away. The thought dies. He stares down at his lap like he's maybe searching for it, the thought. I try to think of the times when we have actually looked each other straight in the eye, longer than just a glance, the smallest recognition before moving on.

We eat some more. Ryan scarfs. But I'm going slow. Like I said, I'm not even hungry. So it's eating just for show. Because I wanted it and now I have to follow through. Not eating would be admitting I couldn't finish what I said I wanted. And there is always the possibility that this will not go unnoticed.

He starts again with: "This is it, though. This is where I come, every day, day in day out, rain or shine. Right here. Where we are right now. I drive, I park, I walk. I take the elevator or sometimes the stairs if I'm feeling a certain way. The same people, the same faces..."

Only he's not talking to us, he's talking to someone else, maybe my mom, maybe just himself, maybe Jim Morrison, who he's always listening to and who my mom says my dad kind of looked like when they were younger and he had long hair down to his shoulders. But he's definitely not talking to Ryan and me.

He's still going: "But when you stop and think about it, what I do, what I'm doing, not just work but more than that, the bigger picture, the facts of it, the grand scheme of things…"

Ryan farts, something he can do, magically, whenever he wants. We wait for a response. But it doesn't come. Our farts, our fighting, our fears—he's a long way from all that now.

"This…"

My father shakes his head. This what?

He's digging for the words, the right words. I'm thinking that he might get there if he keeps going. It's like he's about to break through. But then, no. He stops, pulls back. The words are gone, lost in his throat.

"Your grandfather, my father," he backs up, starting over, "he worked with his hands. With his hands. He helped build homes, buildings, things that mattered." I watch him stare ahead, at the office where he works. "Me, what do I do? What do I do? I process claims forms. I get paper cuts."

He looks at his own hands, like they have let him down, one of many disappointments he's had to live with.

"This is stupid," he finishes, firing up the engine. "This is fucking stupid. This isn't working. I don't know what I was thinking."

Then a pause. He picks his teeth again with the toothpick. Then a little later, after the toothpick has been tossed on the dashboard: "Look. I don't expect you guys to understand this. This is all way over your head. It's complicated. I remember when I was your age, or ages, where I was at then. There's only so much you're capable of absorbing. You're kids still. But things happen. Things change. People have their reasons, okay? People do things. It's just the way it is. And sometimes, most of the time, you don't even know why they did what they did, not until a long time after. Way down the road. And even then, when it's way later, when years have gone by, sometimes you don't know even then, not ever. You just don't know."

And that's it. He stops. He doesn't say anything else, though for a while I think he might. So we finish eating, crumple up the bags, and drive back home. Above us, the sky continues to come to life.

The gas, I want to tell him. We should get gas. He won't make it back to work, no way. But I keep quiet because I know sometimes that's best.

When we get home my mom is up, freaked, saying she was worried like crazy, she just woke up and everyone's gone, what was she supposed to think. Her hair is all tangled and wild and sad, and there are places where it's no longer blonde, patches that are not cooperating. Cigarette smoke sits in the air. She was just about to call the police. Good thing we got back when we did.

"Where were you?" she asks him, not us. But he's walking, in motion, not stopping to make this a full-blown conversation.

"Out," he says. "Out in the world. I wanted to show them something. Now I need to shower and get to work."

"I was worried. First you don't come home till I don't know when. Then I wake up and the boys are gone. I know you've been home at some point because of the empties on the kitchen table and the toilet not flushed. So what—what was I supposed to think?"

But that's it; he doesn't say anything back, just continues his march through the kitchen and heads upstairs and then we hear a door closing. The sound echoes and the three of us stand there and listen to it until it fades and is gone.

School hasn't started yet but it will soon. I get the sense that this could be one of those days where we didn't have to go and my mom writes us a note. She was good at writing notes. They were very detailed. Sometimes she even looked stuff up in medical books to come up with new illnesses and viruses. The people at school seemed impressed by this. Is your mother a doctor or nurse? they asked once. No, we said. What does she do? Silence. Should we or shouldn't we? Ryan took care of it. She works at Photo Barn, he said. Then they were like: Oh, I see.

"What about school?" I ask.

She's pacing in the kitchen in her ratty old-lady robe (she's got a brand-new one, leftover from Christmas, but she's never worn it), the pack of cigarettes showing through the front pocket like always. But she's not smoking. But thinking about the next cigarette, you can tell. And you can tell this, too: She's also been up for most of the night. On her face is the blurry mask of someone who hasn't slept. That, plus the idea—stretching across the forehead, curling around the mouth—that there's some kind of decision being made. Right now. At this very moment. Her eyes are narrowed, focused, like a pitcher eyeing the outside corner of the plate. Her face says, is saying, whatever—it says she's moving from one thing to the next. Today, tomorrow—they would be different. Maybe. Because, you know, I've seen the look before. It doesn't necessarily last.

"What?" she says.

"School," I repeat. "It's starting soon. Are we going?"

"Go upstairs," she tells us. "Both of you. Now. I'm thinking. I'll let you know. I'm thinking."

Upstairs in our room, I can hear the shower running in my parents' bathroom, and right away Ryan dive bombs onto his unmade bed.

"This is fucken bull-twat," he says into his pillow.

I'm not sure what he means: our parents, getting up early, driving to my dad's work, not going to school. Or maybe none of the above.

I want to tell Ryan the dream about the horses but I'm pretty sure he'll say dreams about horses are for wusses—fucken wusses. So I don't.

But I think about the dream again. I try to relive it as I lie down on my bed and close my eyes. I try to get back to that place in my mind when I'm moving and the wind is in my face and things haven't already happened yet and the world spins and shines just for you. It's a long, long time before I open my eyes. And when I do I look out the window. I see that the sun is up and it's completely light outside and I'm only a little bit afraid.

JOB HISTORY

JOB HISTORY

ONE TIME I WORKED as a grocery store bagger. I hated it when people said paper. It threw off my whole rhythm.

My shift was almost over when I heard "Clean up aisle six" mumbled over the loud speaker, and when I got there with my wheeled blue bucket and gray mop, there was puke everywhere. I'd never seen so much puke. A kid was kneeling down, pointing at it. The mother was saying, "Don't touch, don't touch. Let the man clean it."

Another time I worked at a dentist's office. I did the molds for people's teeth. Me and this other guy (Dave? Daryl?). We got through it by getting high in the mornings. We'd sneak out to the alley. Then we'd do the molds. It was summer and ninety-five degrees in the room where we worked and Black Sabbath ruled.

The dentist fired Dave/Daryl after he was late four days in a row and then it was just me. The dentist asked if I thought I could handle everything by myself. When I said sure, he asked if I'd considered a career in dentition.

And then there was the time I delivered telephone books. My trunk loaded down with yellow and white pages, lugging plastic bags through neighborhoods with chained dogs and scorched lawns. That only lasted three days.

My job now is different. Yet the same. I'm married. I have kids. Blah blah blah. These are just the facts.

At night, after my son and daughter are bathed and in bed and the house is once again ours, my wife asks me questions. She asks if I'm restless.

"No," I say. "I don't think so. Not restless. Not that."

"You seem restless. Is it work? How was work today?"

My wife has her own tortured job history—mall jobs, fast-food jobs, office jobs. Her current boss may be hitting on her. We're still analyzing everything he's said and done since she started working there, three months after she got laid off from the daycare place.

"No," I say. "It's not work. Work is just work. Blah blah blah. Can we talk about something else please?"

"Okay," she says.

I am maybe paying a bill, or thinking about paying a bill. The sprinklers on in the backyard, the long, slow descent of water.

And then we talk about something else, and I feel better, and I think my wife does, too.

It's just a matter of convincing yourself, one way or the other.

SOLO ACT

SOLO ACT

THE CLASSIFIED AD THAT Kenny ran, which was how we all met, mentioned bands like Green Day, Nine Inch Nails, the Sex Pistols, the Replacements, Fleetwood Mac, ABBA, and Parliament, plus a few others I'd never heard of. We refused to label ourselves, but if you had to lay a reductive classification thing on us you could do a lot worse than heavy post-punk pop industrial garage funk. Our foundation: juxtaposition and rage.

It was the thick of summer, and the Arizona sun was like kryptonite, making everyone weaker, stupider. Motivation became an issue. We kept at it, though, working nights at our respective wage-slave service-industry jobs in and around Scottsdale—delivering pizzas, barbacking, enduring the graveyard shift at 24/7 Video—while during the day we'd sweat through practice, playing three-chord songs like "I Wanna Be Your Dog" and "Wild Thing" over and over. The band didn't have a name, but we weren't worried. There wasn't any hurry. We were all in our early twenties, sliding because we could.

We practiced at Brandon's apartment complex, Sunscape Apartments, which everyone called Shitscape, and rightfully so. It wasn't the kind of place where you'd ever picture yourself living—the depressingly drab beige and dark brown color scheme, the serial killer building manager, the neglected landscaping, the broken laundry facilities, the chlorine that burned the shit out of your eyes if you dared to swim in the pool— but what could you do? The inhabitants said little, kept low profiles, like parolees not wanting to draw attention to themselves.

One late night/early morning we sat holding court around the pool after we'd all gotten off work, shirts off, pounding our MGDs, wondering, vaguely, what "cold-filtered" meant anyway, and debating, even more vaguely, which Darren was better on *Bewitched*. Then Brandon swallowed a sizable gulp of hops and barley, burped, and said, "Hey, check out the naked chick on the bike."

And we turned to behold just that: a naked girl navigating her way (drunkenly, or druggily, or both) through Shitscape's network of cracked sidewalks and gravel paths on an old Schwinn ten-speed. She was pretty hot in an obvious, porn star kind of way, and older, maybe twenty-eight. She was also pretty royally screwed up. Psycho mom. Incarcerated brother. Broke. In heavy debt. Credit cards maxed. She'd gotten so many DUIs they'd finally taken away her driver's license. So she had to rely on a bike—a bike, in this eyeball-splitting desert/ retirement community heat—for transportation.

She had temporarily moved in with her aunt, another lowly Shitscape resident, to "chill" and "reevaluate" and "figure shit out." Because she couldn't drive she'd been forced to quit one of her part-time jobs: dancing at The Lasso over in Tempe. There were rumors, too—about a kid and some trouble in Albuquerque, among other things. We found all this out later, as the summer stumbled on.

She rode past us on the other side of the pool, a streak of flesh and spokes and nipples. Briefly, the aroma of peaches and cream cut against the water's primordial, sludgy stench. Then the brakes let out a scrotum-curling squeak and she halted in front of a Coke machine, inspecting her choices. Suave fucking dudes that we were, we tried to be as subtle as possible about our collective gawking (but how could we not stare?), speculating where the change would come from, knowing that the machine would yield only Diet Sprite no matter which button you pushed. In the moonlight, naked and wet like she'd just exited the shower, she resembled some kind of—I don't know—goddess, I suppose, a vision from dreams or movies or music videos or the Playboy Channel. At the time none of us had what you'd call girlfriends.

"You saw her first," Alex told Brandon, who had just popped open another beer and was rolling the can across his forehead like in a TV commercial.

"Yeah, so?"

"So go on over and talk to her. Tell her you're a rock star."

More prodding, more coded masculine encouragement, and Brandon lugged over to the Coke machine and the naked girl.

The very next day she started coming to our practices in the Shitscape rec room. Lips perpetually glossed. Eyelids forever shadowed a sultry, supermodel blue. There was immediate tension. She made suggestions. Wouldn't Alex's voice sound better if he wasn't singing through my bass guitar amplifier? How about an actual guitar solo every now and then instead of just chords?

We nodded like idiots. Then we turned up the amps louder, played harder. We—that is, everyone except Brandon—did our best to ignore her, which wasn't easy because of the knit tube tops and spectacularly tan legs, along with the tattoo of a flaming sun that orbited the smooth expanse of her equally spectacular stomach. Brandon seemed embarrassed at first, plucking errant notes on his guitar to fill the uncomfortable silences that followed one of her critiques. As he and Clarissa hung out more and more, watching pirated cable and smoking coma-inducing amounts of Clarissa's aunt's pot, he started to change. It was inevitable—he was a sweet, mellow, mumbling guy who slept until two in the afternoon and never missed an episode of *South Park*. Now he was worrying over his abs and whether or not his goatee was holding him back professionally, musically.

One afternoon Brandon showed up at practice late, clean-shaven and without Clarissa or his guitar. We were jamming on a Led Zeppelin (or was it Jethro Tull?) riff.

Brandon signaled for us to stop.

"There's something I need to say," he said. "To everyone. All at once. If you got a sec. If now would be okay."

This was weird. Brandon was the quiet one. I was, by default, the smart one. We didn't really have a cute one.

Delivering the news like a child who's been instructed by a parent to apologize for lying or stealing, he said, "I'm not being allowed to fully express myself in the band."

We all looked at him like what the fuck. Brandon only knew about five songs straight through and still hadn't figured out how to tune his guitar. I had to do it for him.

"What are you saying, Brandon?"

"What I'm saying is, is I'm leaving the band. I guess."

He paused.

"Sorry," he added.

It was quiet as we absorbed the information: No more rock and roll, which meant the possibility of sex and drugs was greatly diminished. Everything we'd worked not very hard for, gone.

"There's more," Brandon dribbled on, trying to remember whatever Clarissa had scripted for him. "Oh yeah, right. Another thing, another reason why, is we're talking some pretty major creative differences."

Again, silence.

"She's pulling a Yoko," said Alex finally. "I can't believe it. A classic fucking Yoko."

"Or like the chick in *Spinal Tap*," I offered.

The rec room mostly consisted of a ping pong table with no net, a dartboard with no darts. The sound of our instruments sometimes shook the windows, and we kept waiting for them to break, hoping for that kind of actual impact.

"What is it with chicks and fucking up bands," Kenny philosophized from behind his drum kit. His T-shirt said RANDOM INCIDENT, which I'd always wanted to ask him about but never did—another of the world's mysteries left unsolved. "Because it must be, like, in their DNA or something."

Alex unstrapped his guitar and leaned it against his amplifier. A hiss of feedback began to build, slowly birthing to life.

"There's an arc we have to go through first, before this kind of shit can happen," he said. "Rise and fall. Rise and fall. And rise. There's a fucking *arc*."

Brandon fingered the amoeba-shaped hickey on his neck.

"I'm an artist," he explained. "I need to grow."

"Brandon, man, you don't even own your own amp," I reminded him.

"We just think I'd do better by going solo. I been working on some songs, of my own, you know, some darker, edgier stuff. With lyrics and everything."

With lyrics and everything. How could we argue with that?

So just like that we were three, a trio. But with Brandon out of the band, we no longer had a place to practice. And with no place to practice, we could no longer be a band.

Summer ended. Kenny decided to go to school to become a massage therapist, and Alex moved back home, to one of those mini-sized states back east. I lost track of Brandon. As for me, I was thinking about thinking about enrolling for some classes at the junior college. They had a restaurant management program that suddenly seemed worth considering.

The week after classes started (I'd missed the deadline; there was always next semester) I ran into Clarissa at a Taco Bell. She pulled up on her trusty ten-speed, looking very high and very sexy as she parked the bike out front and then stood in line next to me. She ordered some Chalupas.

"How's the band?" she asked.

"You broke us up. You know, so Brandon could be an artist."

Uncharacteristically, she was wearing a shirt that covered her entire stomach. Still it was easy to imagine the sun tattoo that beckoned behind a thin veil of cotton.

"Oh that," she said. "He listened to me too much. That should have been a clue right there."

"Listened. As in past tense?"

"Very past tense. As past tense as past tense can get." She laughed. It was an ugly laugh, a hurtful laugh, a laugh that reduced Brandon down to an inconsequential nub. But damn, she smelled nice.

Clarissa informed me that Brandon was still a boy, a child, and that she wasn't interested in boys, in children, and that she had only one more week left and she'd have her license again, no more of this bike shit, no more Shitscape, no more slumming with the aimless masses. Then she'd be free. She'd get her life back. She'd get back to where she was. She had plans. She'd been reading this great book that said life was like one giant atom, it consisted of Positives, Negatives, and Neutrals, and from here on out it was only Positives. It was all mental, a matter of will, what you thought and decided in your head. Then you made it so. That was the trick. The manager at The Lasso, Dalton, he was being pretty cool about everything and was keeping a weekend spot open for her.

As she talked I realized that, for the first time ever, I was staring at Clarissa's face from up close and not so much focusing on everything below. And there, around the stonily half-shut eyes, you could see where the lines would be, where they were even starting to converge, marking territory, determining who she would be in the years to come.

"You learn stuff about yourself though," she said. "I suppose that's part of the whole point of it, of punishment. That's what the asshole Nazi fuck judge said at least. Being deprived. *You are being deprived, Miss Riley.* And that's what I was all right. Deprived. You ever been deprived—I mean like really, truly deprived, where you wake up in the morning and you know you can't do what you want to do?"

I watched the Taco Bell guy in the back squirting guacamole into our food with a gun-like device. A family of about like fifty picked up a Fiesta Taco Party Platter to go. The kids went nuts, pawing at the mother and the brightly colored bags of food like baby birds, nothing but pure need.

"Not really," I said.

"These past six months or whatever it's been, it's been like living without really living, you know," she said. "Like a ghost. Like one of those Charles Dickinson stories. How about you? Tell me about you. You're kind of cute, you know that? Maybe you already know that. What's your story?"

I thought about it for a while—thought about her naked on her bike, thought about that sun tattoo and what it would feel like against the press of my lips, and how she broke up our band that never even had a name, and how there's probably a sadness behind everything, Taco Bell, certainly, and yes, the end of another summer, the end of something I wasn't ready to face yet. I looked at my left hand, my fretting hand, and right then, right at that moment, I felt like it was capable of wondrous magic despite all that I'd never be, all that I'd never become.

"I'm an artist, too," I lied, but wanting to believe it.

WHY WE CAME TO TARGET AT 9:58 ON A MONDAY NIGHT

WHY WE CAME TO TARGET
AT 9:58 ON A MONDAY NIGHT

DONNIE REMEMBERS JUST IN time. So we run practically every stop sign and red light in town, and get there right before they close. They're about to lock the front doors but we burst on in like we own the place, the goddamn heirs to the Target fortune, telling the puny Rent-a-Cop guy, It's cool, it's cool, we'll be real quick, no worries T.J. Hooker. Then we prowl the aisles, through Home and Living, then Beauty, then Outdoors, and we're laughing, laughing like pirates, and Donnie is still drunk from the Vodka Dews, and I probably am, too, though it's starting to wear off, it's that time where you're crashing faster than you'd like and that feeling of *you can't touch me* is slipping away and you're starting to realize *you can be touched, you can be touched*, no one can escape that sad, basic fact. The puny Rent-A-Cop guy has one of those mustaches that looks like it's been drawn on. And he's shorter than me almost, and Donnie is big, beefy, an all-state wrestler his senior year. So what's the guy gonna do? He doesn't even follow us.

Next Donnie starts pulling stuff off the shelves (deodorant, denture cream, orange-flavored Metamucil), saying, Let's buy this, fuck it, let's buy everything. But I'm not laughing as much now, because I'm remembering why we're here, why we came to Target at 9:58 on a Monday night. I pretend to be real interested in a dress I know I'd never buy. Donnie puts on a bright yellow baseball cap that says Bad Ass. The lights in the store dim (hint, hint). He turns the cap so it's backwards and follows me. Tampons, panty liners, lady things. Then: there. So many to choose from. We should pick a good one, I tell Donnie, who says, How can you tell the difference? It's like fucking cereal there are so many.

They make that announcement where they say the store is closed and you better bring your shit up front and get. Donnie's picking up mouthwash, toothpaste, other crap we don't need. I tell him, Let's go, Bad Ass. And he dumps everything on the floor, including the cap. Some minimum wage slob will have to clean it all up. Not us.

There's a long line to check out. Only one cashier open. The girl who rings us up doesn't blink or bother with hi-how-are-you-did-you-find-everything-you-were-looking-for, she's tired, she wants to go home, she has hair curled and gelled, plus this spooky lipstick and makeup like an old lady but she's not an old lady and should know better.

The drive back is quiet. We stop for the lights. We don't talk. The Vodka Dews have officially worn off. My head spinning like a pukey carnival ride. When Donnie and I first met it was right away. I'd always wanted something like that to happen to me. Then it did. It was both like I'd imagined it would be and also completely different, if that even makes sense. And it was something that got carved into me, something that was mine, something long-lasting and true. I don't want to lose that. I don't want to lose Donnie. He's concentrating on driving, he's squinting, he's leaning forward. Lights flash across his face, fill it with meanings I can't make out, not from this angle anyway.

Say something, I say.

Something, he says.

Come on, Donnie. What are you thinking? The question every boyfriend loves to hear.

What am I thinking? I'm thinking, actually, that my dad's one of those dads. One of those dads who everybody's always afraid of. Like he can explode anytime, anywhere. Push the wrong button and boom. You just never know. I don't want to be like that. I don't want my kid to be afraid of me. That's what I'm thinking.

This sends my heart soaring, it does a little Michael Jackson dance, flutters like a beautiful fucking butterfly.

You won't, I say. You won't be like that.

Suddenly I'm very sleepy, very aware of my body and what could be happening inside of it. Have I gained weight already? Will I start throwing up tomorrow morning? I want to touch my belly but that would be lame.

So what do you think our odds are? Donnie then asks, braking, guiding us into a left turn, the steering wheel sliding slowly back through his hands. Fifty-fifty?

I stare ahead at the road and the lights and the other cars coming toward us, and I gnaw on my lip so hard it almost makes me cry.

Fifty-fifty, I say. That sounds about right to me.

NOT THE L.A. IN MY MIND

NOT THE L.A. IN MY MIND

I KNOW BLOOD. The types, the variations of color and presence and absence. It's what I look at all day long, the way an accountant looks at numbers, the way a butcher looks at meat, the way a painter looks at paint.

Phlebotomist: It was a job that paid well after I graduated from high school, that did not require a college education, that got me out of my parents' house (a mother, a stepfather, no siblings). And it was the first thing I was ever good at. So it stuck. Then I just kept going.

Arms, veins, skin. I don't see faces anymore. The people I see are not people. They are arms, veins, skin. I sterilize. I draw the needle. Insert. Extract what I need. Next.

Because I'm good, I take it personally if I miss the vein, if it takes more than one attempt. The rest of the day, and sometimes beyond, will be tainted by my mistake. I can't let it go.

Phle-bo-to-mist: A lot of syllables, too. Doesn't exactly roll off the tongue, either.

When my coworkers have patients with thin veins or they're having an off day or they have someone with tremors from Parkinson's, they call me in.

"She's our Terminator," they say, and before the patient realizes it, it's over, I'm out, I'm gone, who was that gangly frizzy-haired woman in the white lab coat?

That was me.

"Stab 'em and tag 'em," my coworkers like to joke, but I don't.

•

The lab has its regulars. Lots of people getting chemo who need their blood monitored. Even with them, with these sad, old, bald men and women, I keep my distance. I can't. I just can't.

Today I have a full schedule of appointments, and the waiting room is overflowing with walk-ins. An army of wheelchairs and walkers out there. Complaints about the lack of seats and space and the outdated reading material: copies of *People* and *Sunset* and *O* from three, four years ago. A lone plastic plant in a large pot occupies a corner like it's being punished, a dunce plant. That smell universal to waiting rooms: sterile, chemical, mortal. I call out the name of my next patient. I read names all day and don't remember a single one. Male or female, I don't even notice. The patient follows me back to an exam room. Sits down. Rolls up his/ her sleeve. Arms, veins, skin. Sometimes trying to make small talk, but more often that's not the case. I put out a pretty clear vibe.

But it's hard not to notice the particularities this time. He—yes, the patient is male—is young, and that's fairly uncommon. He has long shaggy black hair, presumably dyed, reluctantly combed. Black T-shirt, black jeans, black backpack slung over his shoulder. A floral tattoo blooms on his left forearm. Pasty vampire complexion. He looks like he could be in a band, or wants to be in a band, or should be in a band. And he's lanky, lean like a tree in the desert. He slouches in the chair, crosses his arms, and stretches out his legs, crossing his ankles as well, like he's the smartest kid in class and isn't having any of it.

He's talking, too.

"So this is what you do, blood," he says.

"Pretty much," I say.

"Nine to five, dealing with blood," he marvels, looking around, surveying the order, the minimalism of the exam room. "That's cool."

"Not really."

"I don't always take my meds."

"Oh. Why not?"

"I don't like to be predictable."

I rub his nontattooed forearm with an alcohol swab, find the vein, massage it gently, noncommittally, with my thumb.

"This won't hurt a bit," I say, which is more than I usually say.

"I bet you say that to all the boys."

He smiles, and I can tell this is something of a rarity for him. The smile seems pained and quickly disappears, back to neutral, back to safe.

Then we're done.

"That it?" he asks.

"That's it."

"Cool. I'll see you next week."

That night I dream about the patient who looks like he could be or wants to be or should be in a band. I don't remember what he says or does, or why here's there. But he is there. He is in my dream. He has crossed over.

My coworkers at the lab are almost all women. Older than me, harder than me, although lately I've been feeling their hardness rubbing off on me—you know, the osmosis thing. They complain about their children and husbands, boyfriends and celebrities. Someone or something is always disappointing them.

The only guy is Salvador. Sal. Rumor has it he's either gay or vegetarian.

"Could he be both?" someone once asked.

"It's possible, I suppose," someone else said. "Anything's possible this day and age, which you could say is one of those Catch-22 deals. Could be a good thing, could be a bad thing, anything being possible. Depends on your life view."

"Life view?"

"Hell. You know what I mean."

"No. I don't know what you mean."

"Well I'm not going explain it now, not here."

And like most conversations at work it soon enough drifted off to another topic, someone started talking about something else, the phone rang, there was an emergency, a sample got mixed up, the UPS guy came, something. And the now-dead conversation never got resolved.

•

During the week that follows, I find myself thinking about the new patient way too frequently. Why? Why this person? He's probably a year or two younger. Several inches shorter than me. Mildly reminiscent of an actor whose name I can never remember. Not someone I would ever conjure in my mind.

But he doesn't come back that week. I return to my apartment at night, thinking about him. The heat arrives. Temperatures hovering near one hundred. Fires farther north, one in Santa Clarita and another in Santa Barbara. One evening I visit my mother and stepfather, my monthly trip to Norwalk, a short drive from Whittier. The house is smoky, cough-inducing, cluttered. You have to move something if you want to sit down.

My mother tells me, in great detail, about her latest urinary tract infection. She explains how she had called her Internet company to complain about a price increase and now she believes they are purposefully slowing down her Internet service. Randall can't enjoy his nature videos as much anymore. There's lag. The videos help him fall asleep at night.

Toward the end of the visit, after we've covered ailing family, annoying neighbors, and even more annoying actors and actresses, she informs me that she will not, as planned, be retiring next year. She can't afford it. She'll be working at least another five years, maybe more.

"I may never retire at this rate," she says, lighting another cigarette. "Randall's 401(k) has been practically wiped out. The bills aren't going anywhere, we're not going anywhere. Just so you know: There's no nest egg here. Don't be counting on that. Just to be clear. We don't live in that kind of world anymore. You work hard all your life and this is what you get."

On Friday, it's someone's birthday. We have cake, sparkling cider. Primarily middle-aged people holding paper plates and using plastic spoons because there are no more forks. I haven't told anyone my birthday. They never ask.

My last patient of the week says she's afraid of needles. Without realizing it, I put my hand on her shoulder. The patient is a woman. I notice.

"This won't hurt a bit," I say. "Promise."

My annual job performance review: I am highly skilled. I am admired by others. I am seen as a potential leader. Coworkers value my input. They would also like to see more of this, for me to be more communicative, less solitary. We are a team, after all. It would be nice if I embraced that more. I sign a piece of paper, agreeing to all this. It's the same as last year and the year before, the same as it's been the past six years. Except that now I get an extra vacation day.

*

I call out his name the following Tuesday afternoon, and he's there this time. He takes a seat in the exam room. My hands are trembling. Why? How am I going to do my job and extract his blood?

"I missed you last week."

Had I said that? Had I meant *missed* as in *our paths did not cross as expected*, or *missed* as in *missed, longed for, was dismayed by his absence*?

"I told you I don't like to be predictable. Ouch."

"Sorry."

"Last time I didn't feel a thing."

"Sorry. I'm trying another vein."

"Do people usually watch?"

"What?"

"Watch the needle go into the arm, accept the pain, embrace it, or look away, close their eyes, pretend it's not happening?"

"I never really noticed."

"You could run with that: 'There are two types of people in the world, people who watch their blood being taken out of them, and those who look away.'"

"There. All done."

The last time I didn't find the vein on the first probe was over a year ago. My streak has ended.

"Are you from here?"

Another first, asking a patient a personal question.

"No, I'm from somewhere else. The other side of the country. I came here because my grandmother lives here and it was Los Angeles and I had expectations and I needed somewhere to go. I didn't realize Whittier was Whittier."

"Not what you expected?"

"Not the L.A. in my mind. That's for sure. Suburbs are suburbs. I could be anywhere."

"There's downtown Whittier, the older part. That part's a little different. They got brick buildings and stuff."

"All I see is Chevron, Starbucks, McDonald's."

"What would you like to see?"

"Something that's not this."

When we're finished, Trevor—that's his name, Trevor—asks if he can stay a while.

"Here? In the exam room?"

"Yeah, here with you. For a few more minutes. It was so quick."

"Well, okay. Just a little while, though. There's a waiting list."

"A lot of people need to have their blood taken. Job security, right?"

"I guess."

"Are there ever times when you just don't want to go to sleep?"

"What do you mean?"

"When you know you should shut your eyes and sleep but you don't? You just keep reading or watching TV or whatever, or thinking, and somehow it makes you more alive than you usually are, during the rest of the regular day?"

"No. I don't think so."

"I'm on one of those jags right now. Not sleeping much. Thinking a lot. Making progress in a bigger picture way. Do I need to go now?"

"Probably."

"All right, he says reluctantly. Until next time, Sylvia."

"How did you know my name?"

"Your nametag."

Right. I wear a nametag.

Later, getting close to my last scheduled appointment of the day, I call out the name Mary Hornbach. An older woman shuffle-walks toward me. She is white-haired and fragile like balsa wood. Liver spots have fully colonized her hands. No going back.

"They want to start me on radiation again," she confides as I prepare her. "But my white cell counts have to be higher. I don't know if I can do it again, the radiation. It feels like your bones are being ground to dust."

"I'm sorry."

"Me too. I just hope the counts stay low. Do what you can, okay?"

I take her blood. Whatever Mary Hornbach wants, she should get. I hold her hand and tell her I hope the counts are low, too. I'll do my best.

A few months ago, we were instructed to call patients *clients*. You didn't help a *patient*. You helped a *client*. This was after the lab was purchased by a larger company, VitaCorp, spurring rumors of layoffs and closures. The speculation has since died down, though, and no one calls patients *clients*.

There is a wraps place, California Wraps, a chain, two blocks away from the lab and decent, and once a week, on Wednesdays, I go there for lunch instead of consuming my yogurt and carrots and leftover tamales in the break room. I order the same food, drink the same drink. Habits are comforts. And my comforts are rare, so I try not to feel too guilty about them. Because it's still blazingly hot today, I drive.

He's sitting on the sidewalk, crisscross-applesauce, camped out to the left of the entrance, writing in a notebook, his backpack open and leaning against him, outfitted in his usual uniform of contrarian black.

"Hey, it's the blood girl. I almost didn't recognize you without your white jacket. Do they make you wear those?"

"It's not optional."

The Radio Shack next door has closed, which I didn't know about until now. There's a note posted in the store window, thanking customers for their twenty-three years of support.

"I get it," he says. "The jacket gives a certain effect, for sure. All official, all medical-ly. You interested in buying me lunch?"

We go inside California Wraps and I buy him lunch. He devours a Corleone Italian Wrap, chips, and a chocolate chip cookie the size of a small baby's head. I offer him the rest of my Sea Breeze Salad, and he eats that, too.

"Do you want to know why I'm coming in to have my blood drawn?"

"It's up to you."

"It's boring."

"You don't have to."

"Everything's boring. Especially the truth. But the truth is, I've got this rare blood disease, one of those one in a million deals, lucky fucking me. I found out last year, before I moved out here."

"I'm sorry."

"I have to get transfusions every once in a while. It's called PNH. Stands for paroxysmal nocturnal hemoglobinuria."

"Okay, wow."

"Basically my red blood cells break apart like prematurely, and there's hemoglobin in my pee. And so one of the dangers of that is blood clots. Thrombosis. The shit I'm learning. It can also mess up your bone marrow."

He pauses, which is something he doesn't do often. I notice a trace of little-boy-ness still informing his face, or at least I can picture him as a boy, riding his bike, swimming in the summer, bliss in his world-greeting expression before something else took over.

"Sorry. That's kind of heavy. And here we are just eating our lunch on a Wednesday afternoon."

"That's all right. I'm glad you told me."

"Have you ever been to The Knight's Inn?"

"No."

"It's a bar. They do music there sometimes. Rebel Yell is playing there tonight."

"Oh yeah?"

"It's a Billy Idol tribute band. The guy sounds just like Billy Idol."

"Cool."

Had I said *cool?* Yes, I had.

"I need to get going. And I'm sure you've got blood to take. Maybe I'll see you there? Thanks for the food and everything. I'll pay you back."

"You don't have to."

"I will. I'm good for it."

"I saw you writing something. In a notebook. When I first saw you."

"Lyrics. Or a poem. I can't decide which. Maybe it's both. I just like to write shit down."

"Cool."

Yes. I said it again.

✳

The sign actually says Ye Olde Knights Inn. The singer for Rebel Yell is well past fifty, also weighing at least fifty pounds more than Billy Idol. Wearing leather and sneering and jumping around on the small stage like a spring coming unwound. What is obviously a wig, blonde and spiky. He could be Mexican. But his voice is just like Billy Idol's. He's got that down. At the bar I order a vodka tonic. Then another. I guess it's my drink, because it's always what I order at bars, even though I've never made this concerted, seemingly important decision. I find myself wondering: Had he been waiting for me in front of California Wraps or was it a coincidence? Purposeful or random? Fated or pure chance? And can you ever know the difference? I don't see any sign of Trevor, and I wait and sip, sucking on melting ice cubes, at the bar, at a table, talking to no one, and when the band starts playing "White Wedding" for the third time I leave.

•

"I'm sorry," Trevor says when I draw his blood again. "I went to take a nap and then I fell asleep. I'd been up a long time. I'm really sorry. How was Rebel Yell?"

"He sounded just like Billy Idol."

"Told ya."

These past weeks I've gotten to know his blood better than anyone else's. It's velvety red, full bodied, hypnotic. I hold the vial and examine it longer than I do the other vials, the other blood I contend with every day. What can it tell me? What can it show me?

He notices me staring, and I feel my cheeks and chest surge with my own variation of red. I label the vial, sign the paperwork.

"I don't think I can stay at my grandma's anymore."

"You're moving?"

"Maybe. Maybe San Francisco. Maybe Portland. Somewhere where there's more soul. It's not really my grandma's place, per se. It's her storage space. Storage America on Whittier Boulevard. A few months after I moved out here, she fell and broke her hip. My parents had to put her in a home and so all her shit had to go into storage and I had to move out. So: Storage America. Did you go to school for this? I keep meaning to ask."

"There's training, a certification process."

"And you get the white coats."

"Yes."

"Maybe you can get me one some day."

Everyone at work receives an email. About half of us are instructed to go to conference room A, the other half to conference room B. There's been talk of naming these rooms for years, something more original and catchy than the first two letters of the alphabet, but no one has ever come up with anything. So: A and B.

"My name is Gloria Jenkins," says a woman we've never seen before, "and I'm your HR representative for VitaCorp. The rest of your coworkers are in another room, being told of some organizational changes. If you are in this room, if you are here now, you are not affected by these changes."

Gloria Jenkins continues to talk for another five minutes, offering details and reassurances and guidance on how to interact with our affected coworkers, and when she asks if anyone has any questions, none of us asks any.

People in conference room A have kids, families, houses, responsibilities. I have none of these things. Yet I am in conference room B. Salvador, Sal, gay or vegetarian or both, is in conference room A.

We disperse without comment. We get back to work, take more blood, there is always more blood, empty glass vials waiting to be filled.

*

But he doesn't show up the next week or the week after that, and I am—what? Forlorn. A word I've never used to describe myself before, and maybe never will again, but it feels right at the moment: Yes, I am forlorn.

People come, people go, entering and exiting our lives, beckoning us, whispering here, whispering there, and it's up to us to listen or not listen. There's the belief that we are nothing but atoms (or molecules) adrift in space, and everything is arbitrary. This seems right to me. So anytime we collide with another atom (or molecule), and there's impact, definite impact, definite touch, we should be grateful, there should be gratitude for and acknowledgement of this small—that is, large—miracle. This also seems right to me.

On Saturday morning, I try to sleep in but it doesn't work out. Veins of sunlight stretch across my sheets, the heat of the day already beginning to assert itself. My apartment is quiet, except for the occasional footsteps above me: a couple that goes to the gym together, who shop at Trader Joe's together, whose names I don't know. It's disconcerting to live so close to them, only a few feet away, and not know who they are. They once had a party and Guns N' Roses blared until two a.m., "Sweet Child O' Mine" playing over and over, as if the song would provide a vital clue if played enough times.

After lying here for an hour, I give up and get out of bed. Laundry, errands, other weekend occupations await. I will call my mother to tell her I won't be coming over and Randall will answer and there will be that long pause as she dramatically walks to the phone, all this effort on my account. I will hear the lighter spark, ignite. I will not ask why I wasn't allowed to attend birthday parties when I was a child. I will not ask why Randall or how come she doesn't talk to her sisters. I will allow her, temporarily, her platform to voice her latest disappointments and grievances. She is like an isolationist country that knows no other way to be.

"Hi," I say to the guy working at Storage America.

"Can I help you?" he replies in a voice that clearly does not want to help me or anyone else.

"I'm looking for someone. He has a storage space here. Or his grandmother does, and he's kind of staying there, or living there, I think."

"You mean Vampire Guy?"

"Yeah."

Storage America Guy looks like he just woke up, even though it's two-thirty in the afternoon. A giant can of Rockstar Energy Drink is within reach on the counter, behind which he stands, tall enough to be a basketball player, an elongated E.T. neck and a significant slouch.

"The payments hadn't been made in months," he says. "We had to kick him out. Plus it's like illegal to live in a space anyway. So we locked him out and then he got all jacked up about it and threw a stapler. Legally the stuff is ours if you don't pay. You sign that shit away. But people don't read the fine print when they sign the agreement."

"He was just living in there?"

"The owner doesn't give a shit. But then sometimes he does. It's hard to figure."

"Did he say where he was going? Did he leave anything behind?"

"Whatever's in the space. Like I said, he was locked out. You can take a look if you want. Take what you want. We're getting rid of everything tomorrow."

The smell inside the storage space hits you hard: musty and farty, that of a trapped body slowly secreting its regrets. Trevor had laid out a sleeping bag toward the back of the space, which is roughly twelve-by-twelve and overrun with boxes, an old dresser, a hanging mirror, a few framed paintings (boats, ocean, sunlight), a stack of photo albums, a vacuum cleaner, rolled up throw rugs, garbage bags full of clothes and shoes and household appliances. All very old and grandma-y, so I assume everything belongs to his grandmother. Next to the sleeping bag (you have to skirt the left wall to reach it) is a line of prescription bottles, three in all; I pick them up one by one: something for his red blood cells, but also Abilify and Wellbutrin. Inside the sleeping bag I find a notebook.

I flip through the notebook, one of those spiral ones like you use in high school. The pages are filled with doodles and sketches, ramblings and descriptions. One entry narrates his trip from Pennsylvania to California and describes the people he encountered along the way—a diabetic out-of-work farmer named Norm, a woman named Vanessa who claimed to be related to Dick Cheney—and another outlines an idea for a movie. It takes place in the future, and it's about a young man who refuses to take the pill that everyone in this futuristic society is forced to take, and after the description there's a line in all caps, underlined, that says: HAS THIS ALREADY BEEN DONE BEFORE? SOUNDS FAMILIAR. NEED TO CONFIRM. IS IT EVEN POSSIBLE TO HAVE AN ORIGINAL IDEA ANYMORE? HOW CAN YOU TELL, VERIFY? ALSO NEED TO CONFIRM. On one of the last pages, I read this: "Went to the blood place, met a girl."

The notebook almost falls out of my hands. There I am. In the notebook. There. Me.

Went to the blood place, met a girl.

I was the girl in "met a girl." I doubt that's ever happened before, but there it is in Trevor's chaotic, childish handwriting. It stuns me. Such a simple thing, but it's like all of a sudden, there I am, placed in the world, seen, remembered.

I decide to take the notebook with me. Also the pills. Then I pull out the white lab coat from my purse and drape it over the sleeping bag where his body would be. I imagine the shape of his body there, inside the jacket. I imagine where he could be, right now. I'm thinking: on a bus, on a train, in a car, in motion, somewhere else, away from here, away from me.

"Thanks," I say to Storage America Guy on my way out. "And he didn't say what he was going to do, where he was going to go?"

"Nope. He was too busy throwing the stapler."

"Do a lot of people end up leaving stuff behind like that?"

"You wouldn't believe."

My apartment darkens and I don't flip on the lights. It is still Saturday and tomorrow is Sunday. Somehow I'll fill the time until I go back to work on Monday. Since there are less people, there is more work. But no one complains. For so long I've thought of my job as a calling. But now I'm not so sure.

I turn on the Addiction Channel and it's that show about addicts who also have the names of famous people: Michael Jackson, Tony Bennett, Julia Roberts. There's a person about my age named Jackie Kennedy who's confessing how she hid her heroin use from her mom for years. "I was surprised," the woman says, "at how good I was at secrets, at telling lies. I was kind of proud of it, actually. I almost got as much of a high from that as I did from the drug."

The notebook sits on my lap, the pills on the end table next to the sofa.

It doesn't necessarily have to be a man, another person, but I guess that's often the case, the cliché. Someone comes into your life and everything feels different after, skewed in a significant way, a good way. It could also be a trip, a book you read, a movie you see. Or a health scare or a family secret or a spiritual epiphany. But usually it's a person who gets you to this place of openness and awakening and renewal, and sometimes that person continues on with you and sometimes they don't. You are alone again but you have seen the possibility of not being alone. Just to know that I could get that close—that was enough, that was a start.

Finally I switch on the lights so I can read the notebook again. A man in a diner in Yuma, Arizona who cursed out the waitress because she reminded him of his ex-wife. A dismissal of his parents, of all the zombies out there, the United Drones of America. He's scared that he has this disease, this thing he'll have to carry through the rest of his life, which will be a shortened life, a marked life. Bob Dylan is overrated. The Beatles are underrated. Squeaky Fromme was part of the Manson family. The vapor trails left behind by planes certainly look different these days, the white exhaust lingering longer in the sky, but he doesn't believe in the conspiracy theories about chemtrails. You have to be vigilant about your defiance. It's so easy to give in, give up.

Did he know the impact he had? Maybe he's already forgetting me, or has completely forgotten me. But then: *Went to the blood place, met a girl.* Maybe—in San Francisco, in Portland, somewhere—he will think of me, wonder what if, wonder about the possibilities like I am now. There is so much that is beyond me, an ocean of mystery and uncertainty. So much water in which to swim. Or not swim. And there is no more nest egg. We don't live in that world anymore. Did we ever?

The name on the prescriptions: T. Niederbach. I remove one pill from each bottle. The first is small, white, round, efficient; the second even smaller, a soothing baby blue, more rectangular. In my hand, they look magical. Like magic beans in a fairy tale. I swallow them and lie down on the sofa, then wait for the effect, wait for the difference.

THE BIG EMPTY

THE BIG EMPTY

WE TOOK THE KID. And I know how bad that sounds, really, I do, but believe me: He was sitting by himself at the gas station, out in the back by the bathrooms and dumpsters and stacks of greasy cardboard boxes, and when Jim came out of the men's room, all sweaty, looking like he might hurl (he didn't), and we started heading back to the car, there he was—this kid, by himself, sitting with his knees tucked up tight against his chest and his head leaning sideways, cheek resting on his knees like he was trying to fall asleep and dream his way out of where he was. I remember thinking: Am I seeing what I'm seeing? There was no one there with him. No sign of parents or brothers or sisters or anybody. He was alone, forgotten, and seemed like he was used to it.

So it was just us and the kid. Waiting there. And the heat—the soul-sucking, melt-your-brain, make-you-stupid Arizona desert heat. We glanced around. No other cars, no other people, nothing. It was August and unforgiving. The bright light burned right into our bloodstream. We had to get inside the car soon or we'd fry.

I tapped him on the shoulder. He raised his head, slowly. And even then, when I saw his round little boy face for the first time, I didn't know how old he was because I've never been good at estimating the age of children. It's just one of those gaps that you know you have and you move on.

"Are you with someone? Do you have anyone?" I asked, but he didn't answer.

Once we were in the car, the A/C cranked as high as it could go without causing the engine to choke, Jim asked, "How old are you?" The kid thought about it for a while and then said, "Pikachu." So that didn't help.

He didn't say anything else after that. We'd ask a question, get no response, wait a while, drive some more, fiddle with the radio, pass the pipe, pop another Tecate, then ask another question. Do you have a mom? What about a dad? Did somebody hurt you? Who left you at the gas station? Where were you born? Do you like cartoons? All kids like cartoons, right?

He was probably older than four. But no more than seven. He had these big blurry brown eyes. As we asked the questions he just looked out the window, just looked and looked, like he was watching a dumb movie out there, out in the desert, the dirt, the sky, the sun, the big empty we were passing through.

"What are we going to do with him?" Jim asked finally.

I didn't answer because I didn't know.

We kept driving. Heard the same Eagles song on two different radio stations. Then we stopped for some food. In the drive-thru line we asked what he wanted. But surprise, he didn't answer. He just stared and stared. Those eyes. What did they know? What did they see?

"Get him a kid's meal," I said. "That's what kids get, right? And they come with a toy. He can play with the toy."

We blasted through the heat, more driving. We were on our way to see Jim's mother. She lived in San Diego and was maybe dying and had some money. The idea was to get back in her good graces. A few years ago, Jim had said some things. Now he wished he hadn't. "You never know," he told me after he said we were making the trip, from Tucson to San Diego, the middle of summer, and I didn't really have a choice because I'd let too much go at that point. "You just never know, Cyn. Lesson learned."

But the kid: he started crying. This after about, I don't know, three hours or so, when I'd almost forgotten about him. Not crying with sound. But crying quiet. We looked at him in the backseat and saw the tears streaming down his face. Sad tiny rivers that didn't know how to stop.

"Jesus," said Jim. "He's crying. I can't take it."

We pulled off at the next town, found a Laundromat. That seemed as good a place as any. It was empty, but dryers dried and washers washed. Someone would be along soon to claim their clothes.

The kid didn't complain when Jim said it was time to hop out of the car. He stood in the Wash N Go and waited. He was no longer crying.

"We should put a note on him," Jim said.

"What?"

"A note. Write something. To explain."

I went back to the car and looked for a pen. Instead there was a crayon in the glove compartment. I don't know how or when it got there, but there it was, a goddamn crayon, magenta or some shit. It was partly melted, but I tore off a piece of our California map and managed to smear something that was halfway legible:

WE FOUND HIM. WE DIDN'T KNOW WHAT TO DO. WE TRIED. HE DOESN'T TALK MUCH. SORRY.

After, we felt bad. Then later, we felt a little better. Then after that, we felt a little worse.

"We did the right thing," said Jim. "Us? Parents? I don't think so."

It was dusk by then, the sky all dramatic and filled with colors that don't have names, and we probably had four more hours of driving ahead of us. Jim and Cyn. That always made us laugh. That made us think it would last. Eventually we'd discover that Jim's mom had moved. We never found out where.

"You're probably right," I said, looking out the window and wondering what he saw out there in the desert, the kid who was somewhere between four and seven and who would haunt my dreams for years to come, one of those mysteries that stay with you and fuck with you and make you question everything you've ever done.

Neither of us spoke for a long time. And it wasn't until we hit El Cajon that I said what I'd been wanting to say for miles:

"We should probably call the cops or something."

Jim shot me a look like *yeah right* and turned back to the road, concentrating, focusing on the thing he hoped would soon be there in front of us—a sign, a warning, an ending, something.

"People like us don't call the cops," Jim said.

And he was right.

MY STATUS

MY STATUS

Pictures don't lie. And there I am, in a photo that's now prominently displayed on the fridge, among the magnets and coupons and crazed crayon drawings of my eight-year-old son. It took a while to recognize myself. Then it was like: *Oh shit, that's me.* Bloated, drunk, ugly, looking like a man who's made an all-star career of letting people down, including himself. Damn. Is that really me? Are my eyes really that close together, that guilty? And how long has the photo been up? I don't live here anymore, so maybe it's been a while and I just haven't noticed it until now, here to pick up my son. Every other Saturday is the agreed upon arrangement. That's when I'm still a dad.

I close the refrigerator door, a Diet Rite Cola in hand. Julie's doing something by the sink, her back to me. She doesn't turn around until she hears the *pssst* of the can opening. I picture myself stewing about the photo and saying nothing for weeks and weeks, letting it become a bigger deal that it actually is, but no, not this time: I'm going to say something right now.

"New addition to the fridge," I say, casually, like it's no big deal, before I take a sip of the Diet Rite. The fizzy carbonation floods my nostrils. "Nice touch," I add. "Really ties the room together."

Julie wipes her brow with her arm. I see now that she's been scrubbing the sink. She's wearing red rubber gloves and looks pretty good—at least pretty good for it being Saturday morning and taking care of housework and sweating and working all week and managing to hit the happy hour at Black Angus last night. Her jeans are tight and her shirt is tight, something she can still get away with. Strands of wet hair—long desperate streaks—cling to both sides of her face.

121

"It's for perspective," she says, a little out of breath. "Enjoying your complementary beverage?"

"I can put it back. What do you mean perspective?"

The picture is an extreme close-up, also a little out of focus, which makes it worse somehow. I try to pluck it off the fridge but Julie's quick, always has been, one of her trademarks, like high heels and the rose tattoo above her left boob, and she blocks me.

"Like symbolic," she says. "Of before, after."

I get it. I'm the before. And I guess Brad, the new boyfriend, would be the after.

"How about taking it down?" I ask, a reasonable request.

"Why would I do that?"

"Come on, Julie. I look like crap. The kid's going to see it all the time, every day. It doesn't even look like me. It's like a different person."

The photo has some history. There's no memory of Julie taking it, or of the specifics that led up to the moment I was captured. Just haze. Another long weekend, another round of ultimatums and declarations. It seems like the photo was taken years ago, but it's more like months. After Julie got it developed, she put it under my pillow. I woke up one morning and felt it underneath. I looked at the photo, groaned, then tossed it on the floor, thought nothing of it again until I was confronted with this grotesque reflection of myself on the refrigerator, which, by the way, has a broken ice dispenser and a cracked crisper.

"Nope, it's you all right," Julie says. "Again, that's part of the point. That's the perspective."

"Ah, I see. You get to have the new life, the new boyfriend, and the going back to school. You get to change and I don't, I can't. Is that it?"

"The weather changes, Cal. People don't. Not you anyways. It's just fact."

I'm holding the Diet Rite and I want to fling the blue can across the kitchen, watch it, hear it smash against the wall. But I don't. That's what I might have done in the past. That's why I'm not living here anymore. And I want to tell Julie, *See? I didn't. I could've. But I didn't. That's change. That's progress.* But I don't say anything. I'm not good with speeches, with words. Yet another thing I'd like to change. The right words at the right time can save you.

"And speaking of facts, let's be honest," Julie continues. "The fact that you're standing here. The fact that I'm still allowing you in here, letting you take our son out. After what you did. Consider yourself lucky. The picture stays."

"All right," I say, setting down the soda can on the counter. "The picture stays."

Why is it that you run into someone from high school just when the other day you were thinking *It's been a while since I've run into someone from high school?* It doesn't happen too often in La Mirada. This particular Southern California suburb is large enough to provide a fairly comfortable level of anonymity. You can blend. You can avoid having to explain yourself to people you don't know anymore. But that's the danger of staying in your hometown: every now and then you see a ghost. Getting gas. Waiting in line at Blockbuster. Or, in this case, shopping at the Trader Joe's up on Whittier Boulevard.

Scott Yoder was known only by his last name back then, one of those guys. And that, plus the fact that he could reliably get pot from his older brother, is about the only thing I could remember about him. He shook my hand like a politician. I had gained weight, achieved little. He had actually lost weight, achieved a lot. He'd married Amber Whitlock, the girl who went to the rival high school and had honey-blonde hair and a tan Mustang—the unattainable dream girl. Somehow Yoder had attained her. I wondered if she called him Yoder. Yoder, let's go out tonight. Yoder, how about Europe this summer instead of Cancun?

"Wow, Amber Whitlock," I said, noticing that his shopping cart was full of things like yogurt, tofu, vegetables, while mine was not full of things like yogurt, tofu, vegetables.

"How about you?" asked Yoder. "What's your...status?"

My "status" was complicated. I was married but I wasn't. I had a son but I wasn't a father. I was supposed to call a lawyer. Julie kept asking about it, the lawyer, the lawyer, the lawyer. I told her I'm on it, that it's on my list. My brother worked with someone who had been through a divorce and said the guy was pretty decent as far as lawyers go, which isn't saying much, I know. But I hadn't called. So that, I guess, was my status.

"It's complicated," I said. "My wife and I, we're going through some stuff. We're separated, actually. For now. But we'll see. We'll see what happens. We just need to turn a corner."

"Sorry to hear that, man. What is it, that statistic—that one out of every two marriages or something fails? But I hope things work out the way they should work out."

"They will, thanks."

"Well good seeing you, Cal. It's been a while. High school was a trip."

Yoder pushed his cart away and got in the checkout line. After he left the store, I added some items to my cart: yes, yogurt; yes, tofu; yes, vegetables. I put back the chips, one of the bottles of Stoli. See? I'm trying. But what the hell do you do with tofu? Now I've got two slabs of the stuff, taking up space in my refrigerator, which, by the way, doesn't have any photos or magnets or anything. It's just white empty space.

The kitchen looks different, feels different. And it's not just the addition of the picture. It's something deeper. I walk over to the cabinet next to the sink to get a glass for some water. I need it after the Diet Rite. I don't usually drink much soda and now I remember why. I open the left door. But that's where the plates are. I open the right door and there are the glasses. Had it always been that way? I could have sworn the glasses were on the left.

"Jagger's getting dressed. He's a slow dresser, you know."

Jagger—I'd lost the battle on the name. I mean, I like the Stones as much as the next guy. But Jesus. Jagger?

"I know," I remind her.

"And if you guys go out to eat, remember, he shouldn't eat pickles. They make him burp like crazy."

"I know, Julie. Just because I don't live here anymore doesn't mean I don't remember things about my son. It hasn't been that long. I haven't lost that many brain cells yet."

Jagger walks into the kitchen, just as I'm finishing that last sentence and my voice rises to an almost-yell. He's wearing a white karate outfit, about two sizes too big for him. He holds up his pants as he walks.

"Hey buddy. That's new."

"Didn't I tell you?" Julie says. "You're taking him to karate today."

"Not karate," says Jagger. "It's Shotokan. That's what Sensei Jerry says to say."

"I didn't know you were into karate, buddy. I mean, what you said."

"It's okay. I'm not."

"There's a waffle in the toaster," says Julie.

He grabs the waffle with one hand, still holding up his pants with the other, and leaves. The TV goes on in the living room, loud. That's pretty much what he does, too, when he comes over to my new apartment. My first day there after moving in all my stuff, which wasn't much, I went into the bathroom, looked at myself in the crooked mirror, and then found a surprise in the toilet. It's hard not to view something like that as a sign.

"Saw someone I went to high school with the other day."

Julie moves on to unloading the dishwasher.

"Yeah? Who's that?"

"Scott Yoder."

"Doesn't ring a bell."

"No reason why it should. We just knew each other, were in the same class. We weren't friends or anything."

"And what's Scott Yoder up to these days?"

"Scott Yoder is doing good. He's doing really good. Living the life. Good job, wife, kids. He's got a boat. They take it up to Arrowhead. They have a place right next to some actress who's in a soap opera or something. He told me the name but I can't remember."

"He's probably lying. What'd you tell him?"

"I told him the truth."

Julie pauses from her dish-putting-away to frown, a frown I know all too well, the left side of her mouth creeping up, up. I'm just standing there, wishing I still had the Diet Rite so I could be holding something, occupied in some small way.

"Why would you do that? That's one of those rare opportunities where you could've said anything, could've said anything in the world. You could've been a doctor, a lawyer, a freaking professional golfer. I would've lied my teeth off. Gave him a good story."

"The truth isn't a good story?"

"Not usually."

"What would you have said then?"

"That I live up in Malibu in this big mansion. That I've got my own business. That my husband is rich and comes from a rich family and treats me like a queen. That my kid is gifted and got skipped two grades. That—"

"You've been thinking a lot about this."

"I think about things, Cal, it's true. Have him back by six, K?"

"I will," I say, and start toward the living room. "You sure about keeping that picture up?"

"I'm sure," says Julie.

What I did was this: I kidnapped the damn dog. Julie's dog, Nibbles, a little Shitzu that she loves more than anything. Things between us had been going down, down, down (sometimes we ignored it, sometimes we didn't), and for whatever reason it was now even worse than usual, and I was sleeping in the living room and supposed to be looking for a place. So I figured, with the help of the Miller Brewing Company, that I could get back in her good graces by being a hero. How could I be a hero? That was a good question. I didn't know. But the idea came to me one night, flipping around the cable channels and scratching off lottery tickets, when Nibbles went on one of his barking jags. Ah-ha! Why not take the dog to my brother's for a few days. Console my wife as she gets upset, cries, etc. Put up missing flyers. Scour the neighborhood. Be a rock. Then, after a couple of days, cruise over to Jeff's and pick up the dog and bring him home, saying I found him hiding near some bushes, shivering, whimpering, poor little thing. I'd save the day! I'd prove myself! So that was the plan. And yes, many beers were involved in the conception of all this, and when many beers are involved in anything, my already shaky judgment tends to get even shakier.

Unfortunately, it all hit a snag when Julie went to our next door neighbor's the day after I'd whisked Nibbles away—yes, there'd been the tears and the consoling, and I had made a flyer on the computer. I was out posting the flyers and supposedly driving around looking for Nibbles. Cheryl, our neighbor, who's divorced and never cared much for me, and who I called Mrs. Kravitz (after the nosy neighbor on *Bewitched*), told Julie that she saw the Nibbler just yesterday, he was barking his head off and Cal was shoving him into his car and Nibbles was barking and barking and then Cal sped away like a crazy man.

After a few hours, I came home. To pad the time, I'd stopped at The Library. Which wasn't a library but a bar called The Library, so when you came home and your wife asked you where you were, you could honestly say, "At The Library." But when I pulled into the driveway, and Julie rushed outside, she didn't ask where I'd been.

"Where is he?" she said. "Where's my dog? What did you do to him?"

So yeah, that didn't go so well for me.

My son stares out the passenger's window. His lips are moving but no words are coming out, he's not saying anything. Just those lips. Maybe he's creating his own language. Maybe he's mouthing sentences that he wants to say to me but can't. His hair falls over his eyes and I want to brush it away. Didn't Julie know he was due for a haircut? He's still not talking. He fiddles with the air conditioning vent. He taps the dashboard like he's checking it for something. He starts to hum. There are things about him that I'd like to know but I have a feeling I never will. My mysterious universe-unto-himself son.

We hit a red light, sitting, waiting.

"Are we talking? Or are we not talking today?"

Jagger's lips stop moving.

"We're talking," he says, looking out the passenger's window again.

"Good. So tell me. What about Brad? What's he like?"

ANDREW ROE

"He wears cologne."

The light turns green. Someone behind me honks.

"You like him? He a good guy?"

"Yeah."

"Yeah? You like him? He a big guy? A big guy like me?"

"I don't know."

"What else? What else about Brad?"

Jagger doesn't say anything for a while and I assume that's the end of the Brad conversation. But it's not.

"He says that people need more love. That it's okay to say you love someone. You shouldn't be afraid. You shouldn't be afraid to say that to people."

"He said that?"

"All the time. And he snores."

"He snores?"

Jagger nods. He looks so serious. He's such a serious boy, an adult from day one, right out of the womb. Often I want to do something—tell a joke, fart, make a face, something—just to try to see if I can get him to crack a smile. They're rare, like eclipses.

Another red light, and the silence deepens. The stereo's broken, so that's not an option.

"So what else, buddy? What's new at school?"

"Nothing. This boy there says he's going to kick my a-s-s."

"Wait. What? Who said that? Which boy?"

Green light, go. Which reminds me of when Jagger first started talking. My mother taught him to say "Red light, stop; green light, go." Except he insisted on saying it as "Red light, go; green light, stop." No matter how many times I tried to tell him that was wrong, he kept saying it, saying the opposite.

"This boy," he says.

I speed up to make a lane change.

"He said kick your ass—I mean a-s-s?"

"Lots of times, yeah. You said ass."

This is what it has come down to. Parenting on the fly: in cars, in lines, on the phone.

"What did you say? What did you say when the boy said he was going to kick your a-s-s?"

"I said why."

"And what'd he say?"

"He said because. And when I asked him again, he just said I'm going to kick your a-s-s again."

Kids can be cruel to kids like Jagger, I know. After all, I did my fair share of tormenting. When I think back on it now, I never picture the kids I grew up with. Instead I picture Jagger. I picture it being my son that I'm making fun of, tripping, giving Hurts, Don't Its to.

"Did you tell your mom?"

"Yeah."

"What'd she say?"

"She said to ask you. Then she saw this flyer at the market. She signed me up for karate. I mean Shotokan."

After two weeks away I thought I was good. I'd learned my lesson, realized that it isn't until after you lose something that you truly appreciate it. You think you have it bad and then you have it worse, and then you know. You know that bad wasn't so bad. It's all about perspective. Like Julie says.

I showed up at the house on a Sunday, thinking that might help my chances. I hadn't shaved for a few days, also strategic, and I hunched my shoulders and bowed my head.

"No way," Julie said. "No way."

All I could think of were stupid clichés, heavily used words and phrases that long ago had lost their power. But they were all I had, so I repeated one after another, without success, unable to convince my wife.

"This time it's different," she told me. "We're not going around and around again. It's different now. It's time to move on, Cal."

But I didn't move on. I went back to my brother's and kept putting off getting an apartment and calling a lawyer like Julie said. Work didn't seem possible, so I called in sick. Then I started letting myself into the house late at night. Usually I just sat on the couch in the living room, just sat and listened and waited. One night I fell asleep. I woke up with Jagger in front of me, those big, brown, little boy eyes that tell you everything in a glance.

"You better go, Dad. Mom's up, too. She'll be right down. She'll be mad."

I kissed him on the forehead and left, vanished like a masked superhero whose identity remains unknown.

And I didn't have any reason to think Julie would take me back— no overtures, no signs, nothing.

But I continued to think it would happen, that it was only a matter of time, of proving myself in some magical, last-minute way.

Sensei Jerry has a lot to say. In fact, he does more talking than showing the kids how to fight and defend themselves. He talks about discipline. He explains how the mind is the most dangerous weapon of all. He quotes from *Karate Kid 3*.

You can tell he's trying to go the Chuck Norris route with the hair and the beard, but he's a little chunky, like me, like he's been slipping on his training, squeezing in one too many chili dogs, and he's got a smoker's cough and skinny wrists to boot. When he finally finishes talking, he goes through some poses and moves with the kids. They thrust and yell and roundhouse kick. Jagger always seems one step behind. He has to keep pulling up his damn pants.

After, Sensei Jerry gives another speech.

"You are strong," he tells the kids, who by now are yawning and rubbing their eyes. "You are courageous. Remember that. What you learn here you take back into your life, your day to day life, everything, all that you experience, and it makes you stronger. It makes you warriors. You're all warriors. Warriors of the mind and spirit and body. And I'm proud of all of you."

Walking to the car, I ask Jagger what he thought.

"I don't want to go back I think," he says.

"You'll have to talk to your mom about that. She thinks it's a good idea."

"I don't think I like it."

I open the passenger door for him, we slide into our seats, buckle up. I look at the streaks of dirt on the windshield. The car needs a wash, an oil change, a tune up.

"All right," I say. "You don't have to go back. Tell your mom I said so. I'll take the heat on this one."

"Okay," says my son.

Then, after I start the car and we pull out of the parking lot, he adds, "Thanks, Dad."

We're both hungry after all that. I'm craving a Tommy's burger, but I don't think my stomach can handle the chili they slather all over it. So we cruise along Imperial Highway and settle on whatever we see first: a Burger King.

We get our food, find a booth in the back. It's still a little early for lunch, so the place is practically empty except for an old man sitting alone, sipping coffee and reading a newspaper and stroking his ancient chin like he's grappling with some great philosophical dilemma. Jagger and I sit down, and here we are, father and son, sharing the joys of fast food and bonding over our burgers and fries and giant sodas. We don't talk much, but this time that's fine. Two weeks ago, on our last lunch outing, it was a different story. We weren't talking, weren't smiling, not sure if we should just put all the food back in the bags and eat in the car as we drove. Now, however, as the place begins to fill up with other people, and Jagger launches into a description of one of his favorite new TV shows (aliens, the future, robots that seem human), we're good with staying. We slow down. We take our time.

Brad's car is parked in the driveway so I have to park on the street. He drives a Prius, a sparkly blue one. Probably listens to NPR and has a Kenny G ring tone. I bet he knows what to do with tofu, too.

Jagger unlatches his seat belt. I hand him the bag with his leftover fries, tell him to take care of himself, have a good week, that we'll talk on the phone in a couple of days. I almost ask him to run inside and take the photo off the fridge. But I don't want to get him in trouble.

Once I'm on the freeway, I call my brother. He's at home, of course. Where else would he be?

"I'm telling you I want that number, that lawyer's number," I say, the words coming quickly. "I'm driving. I'm driving right now. But I'll call back later so I can write it down. I'm calling to tell you I want the number. I want to call that lawyer."

"All right, all right, I got it, shit. You okay? You sound all amped. I thought you were trying to cut back on the booze."

"I'm fine. I just wanted to say that. To be on the record. I'll call you later."

So: I'm on the record. It's official. It feels good but also bad. But mostly good.

I'm still not used to it: being alone, eating alone, everything alone. The quiet. The nothing to do. My apartment doesn't help either. It came furnished, the furniture uncomfortable and brown, sized for a race of tiny people, smelling of Goodwill and potpourri. The type of carpet you think twice about being barefoot on. I heat up my dinner in the microwave I bought at Bed Bath and Beyond. Stand as I eat. TV on. The phone doesn't ring. A few more hours to kill before I can justify crawling into bed and trying to sleep.

Later that night, around two a.m., I wake up and here's what I'm thinking: I'm thinking that someone out there is living the life I should be living. Scott Yoder. Yeah. That should be me.

Without really thinking things through, I get dressed and drive back to the house, Brad's Prius still in the driveway. The street is quiet and peaceful, like it never is during the day. It's strange to stand outside on the porch, look at the house, look at the neighbors' houses (and their cars, their toppled garbage cans), and think I used to live here. Used to: past tense.

I let myself in. No worries about Nibbles, since the dog sleeps with Julie and could doze through a hurricane. It's dark, of course, but pretty soon my eyes adjust to the lack of light. The moon creeps in here and there, everything bathed in a stoney, mellow light. I know what I'm going to do, what I want to do. But I want it to be slow. Slow and significant. Jagger's karate outfit is in a pile at the bottom of the stairs.

In the kitchen, I switch on the light above the stove. I'm about to take off the photo from the fridge but I stop when I see Jagger's crayon drawing first. What is it? What's it supposed to mean? There are monsters, I guess. Or maybe they're half-monster, half-human. Heads come out of arms, arms out of legs, other unknown objects emerge from stomachs. Lines run off the page, colors cross and swirl. I don't get it. I don't understand him, my son, truly I don't, but he's a good kid and he'll be a good man, a better man than I am or will ever be. There's a comfort in that.

Off comes the photo. I leave my key on the kitchen table.

Driving, picking up speed, making all the lights this time, I open the window. The night air leaks inside, cool and vast. It would be dramatic to burn it, I suppose, do something ceremonial. But I've never been dramatic or ceremonial. Instead I try to rip it up. When that doesn't work, I crumple it up, only it doesn't really crumple (what are pictures made of these days anyway?). I just want it to be gone, away. The picture doesn't tell the whole picture. Like the man says, there are two sides to every story, or like another man says, there are three sides to every story: your side, my side, and the truth. But it's me, undeniably me, and pictures don't lie. I need to do better.

It's true what they say about living in Los Angeles: you're always driving somewhere. And here I am, past three in the morning as I hit the onramp for the 605, and once I'm on the freeway, there are cars on the road, always cars. Where are all these people going at this time of the day? We all have our stories, I bet. We all have our reasons.

I don't even look at the photo as I toss it out the window, driving for a long time until it's behind me, behind me, behind me.

WHERE SHALL WE MEET?

WHERE SHALL WE MEET?

SHE GOT STUCK IN traffic. She overslept. She ran into an old friend. The bus was late. The cat was sick and dying and had to be rushed to the vet. She got the directions wrong. She got the time wrong. She lost his phone number and therefore couldn't call him. And she was thinking of him, right now, at this very moment, scurrying like mad, desperate and frantic like in those dreams where you're late and trying to get somewhere but can't, not wanting to blow this opportunity, trying to make it to the café in time, the agreed upon place on Montgomery Street, three days after they met at the party of a mutual friend, introduced, everything aligning just so, finding themselves among a semi-circle of seven or eight people, the topic of conversation ranging from sucky jobs to public transportation horror stories to chemically dependent siblings, the participants dwindling from seven to five to three to just the two of them, a pleasant, natural reduction, the slow ballet of words and gestures, verbal disclosures and withholdings, discovering that they shared the same birthday (a sign!), loved Tom Waits and Kurt Vonnegut (another sign!), the night progressing and expanding like a movie and then ending with a kiss on the balcony, wine on her lips, smoke in her mouth, the taste of cucumber and mint and promise, phone numbers exchanged, the departing and subsequent night of restless sleep, a brief phone conversation the following day (because he couldn't wait, he called, he had to call, he said fuck it to that whole guy credo thing of waiting and making her wonder, and perhaps this was the beginning of the end, no?), him asking "Where shall we meet?" and her pretty obviously caught off guard by the suddenness, it was like coming too fast the first time, this rapid progression throwing her a bit and causing an epic pause, her eventually recovering and answering by saying, "Right, let me think, where would be a good place, you work downtown, right?" and the time and the place decided upon and but she said sorry but she had to go, couldn't talk (another sign?) and now he was waiting and sitting and reading a day-old newspaper, digesting sports scores and financial data he could give a shit about, waiting, not the first time he'd gotten his hopes up like this, sure, he was forty-three and single and saggy and increasingly aware that such encounters were rare and had to be handled carefully, handled like dried flowers or brittle fossils, and he waited, waited, for as long as he could before he finally stood up and felt his legs buckle and then stabilize and then start to move, exiting, he was walking now, leaving the café, the sidewalk filled with the lunchtime crowds, passing many women, checking to see if each one was her, could be her, or even someone else who could still make him believe and start all this again, and they, the women, all seemed to be scarved and beautiful and leaning into the wind, moving much too quickly for him to realize what he was missing.

WHERE YOU LIVE

WHERE YOU LIVE

IT WAS THE DIRECTOR himself who called. His voice sounded serious and low, finely honed, as if trained for such occasions, the delivering of bad news to loved ones and relatives. And this was what he told me: my mother—sixty-eight years old, known for her marble sponge cake and Zen-like bridge skills, a rabid fan of movie musicals—was missing. *Missing.* Though he didn't use that word. Delicate, well-chosen euphemisms were employed instead. "Temporarily unaccounted for" was one, "currently unsupervised" another.

But as strange and unbelievable as it sounded, she apparently vanished from her room at Arcadian Acres. Went AWOL. "Disappeared," as they say in certain Latin American countries, although that usually implies something political, and this wasn't political. Or was it? I mean, what would cause an otherwise docile and resigned senior citizen to flee the security of an assisted living situation when all other feasible options had already been thoroughly examined and re-examined? I suppose it could be a number of things: a protest against society's treatment of the elderly, the onset (finally) of Alzheimer's, boredom, a whim, something she saw in a made-for-TV movie starring Angela Lansbury. Regardless, she ran away. Last seen in her robe, wearing slippers, sans her trusty wig.

"For now I'm classifying it a stage-four moderate," the director explained to me.

I waited. The phone line clicked every five seconds or so. He wasn't going to elaborate.

"Is that bad?" I asked. "A stage whatever?"

When the phone rang I had been in my bedroom. Late morning

ANDREW ROE

but still in bed. Lightnin' Hopkins, that patron saint of the lonely and bluesy, on the stereo. Contemplating the black hole of another Sunday. The blinds closed, but I didn't have to open them to know what the weather was like: gray gray gray. Whenever the sun appears it's like a mirage, something that can't be trusted to last.

"Could be better, could be worse," he said.

"Okay."

"Middling."

"Sorry?"

I'd never actually met or spoken to the director before. According to A.A.'s brochure (featuring glossy shots of well-adjusted white-haired ladies giggling like school girls and an Olympic-sized swimming pool I'd yet to see), he had a Ph.D. in something called Advanced Modern Geriatrics. He also offered a thirteen-part series of motivational learning tapes and interactive CD-ROMs, which were available for a significant discount to the family members of clients. That's what my mother was: a client.

"Middling," he repeated. "If you're after a succinct one-word description, I'd go with *middling*."

I pressed him for more details (it was my mother after all, and fuck, she was *missing*), and he rattled off information and facts like an anchorman reading his lines. A staff person had entered her room (to wake her, help her get dressed, and ensure she took her multiple meds, all of which was very routine, the director assured me) only to find an empty, unmade bed and the TV on. All standard procedures and follow-up were being performed. The director promised to keep me informed of the situation as it developed (again, like an anchorman). When I realized he was about to hang up and leave it at that, I started to stammer. Had the police been contacted? I asked. The director paused and let several seconds of purposeful silence pass, to remind both of us who had the Ph.D. and infomercial contract. At last he said he hoped to avoid jumping to any drastic conclusions and that things would no doubt be remedied in a timely and efficient manner. His exact words: "remedied in a timely and efficient manner."

Clients, the director continued after another prolonged breath,

142

often wander away, especially at night, especially after the holiday season, a time when depression soars. The next day they usually get picked up by the police or a concerned motorist, or they wander back themselves out of fear and hunger and purposelessness. Why bother the authorities, who are busy enough already? I agreed that this was a good point. The director seemed pleased at my concession. Besides, he added, the home had had a recent spat of bad publicity: lawsuits, suspicious deaths, health violations, immigration raids, other disappearances.

"But surely you've heard all about that in the news," he said.

"Yes," I lied.

"Well then I'm sure you understand my situation."

"Yes, of course."

"Good. That's settled then. I'm making a note to make a note of your cooperative attitude."

"Thank you," I said, stupidly. My mother was gone, possibly dead. Why was I thanking him?

"Not to worry, Mr. Ormsby. People don't just vanish into thin air. Here at A.A. the well being of the client is our first and fundamental concern. We'll get to the bottom of this, I assure you. We're not the McDonald's of assisted living facilities for nothing you know."

Before I realized it, I'd thanked him again. And not only that: After I hung up the phone it occurred to me that I'd forgotten to ask a very important question. Namely, when, exactly, had my mother disappeared? The director said that the people at the home usually turn up the next day. Did that mean my mother had disappeared last night? Or could it have happened days ago? There was no way to be sure. I tried to call the home back, but the line was busy. When I finally did get through a half hour later, a woman's prerecorded 900-number voice thanked me for calling Arcadian Acres, a division of the Fletcher Corporation, and said that my call was very important and to please hold for the next available service representative. Then Muzak. Then click. Disconnected.

My last visit was Christmas day, over two months ago. The staff had decorated the home with nothing but strands of shabby tinsel and a handful of skeletal poinsettias. Other guilty offspring lurked about, checking their watches and carrying packages. A group of teenagers from the nearby James Danforth Quayle School for Boys sang carols, bitterly. Most of my mother's brethren appeared tired and skeptical, like they'd given up on the youthful facade of Yuletide cheer and peace on earth years ago. I didn't stay long, just enough time to see my mother, give her a present, and down a glass of watery eggnog.

You could say our relationship is cordial, one of mutual disinterest and tolerance. It's always been that way, even before she went to live in the home, before my father died suddenly, without drama or distinction, the summer I turned twelve and first discovered cannabis and Pink Floyd. I remember him as small, timid, ghostly, marginal; a morsel of a man who kept to himself (we all did) and voted Democrat and slurped his soup. Whenever I encountered him—in the garage, in the kitchen, out on the back porch that looks down into the valley and, on rare clear days, beyond—he always seemed a little surprised to see me, as if I was a foreign exchange student, not his son, and he could never immediately place my name or country of origin. If there was ever a time when he didn't have his own room down in the basement, I couldn't say.

After my father other men lived with us as well: Tom the auto parts salesman, Reg the real estate guy, Jack the investor, Ellis the retired cop. Each one, it seemed, brought more distance between my mother and I, yet another barrier that we instinctively steered ourselves around. They were always wanting to arm wrestle or play one-on-one in the driveway, calling me pussy or fag if I didn't accept their manly challenges. At some point I went to college at Portland State, tried to grow a beard, flirted with Stoicism, developed severe asthma, dropped out with only a semester to go before I graduated, came back home (it was Jack by then, I think), gained twenty-five pounds, and started working at the hospital. Cut to today. That was the vague chronology. There were periods when I drank too much and tried too hard to fall in love. But that was a long time ago.

Eventually the men stopped arriving and departing. It was just the two of us, more like fellow boarders than mother and son. We spoke less and less. I had a TV in my room, she watched in the living room or in her room. Then one night after *Matlock* she fell and broke her hip. She was getting older and more feeble and I was unremarkably approaching thirty. The illnesses escalated. Her bones were weak, lacked density. Cataracts, arthritis, low T-cell counts. Tests, procedures, operations. She heard voices. Her bladder faltered. Insurance was maxed out. There was the time she peed right there on the kitchen floor and began to cry. Something had to be done.

She didn't resist the idea of the home. In fact, she accepted it with great dignity and grace. There were times, however, when it was difficult to tell if she truly knew what was happening. We'd been over everything numerous times, but when I loaded up the car with her belongings and drove her to A.A. she was under the impression that we were visiting a friend.

"You mean I'm staying?" she asked as I unpacked her bags in the sparsely furnished room and then lined the shelves in her closet with a cheery floral-patterned paper. It smelled like cat piss in there, despite the no-pets rule.

"This is where you're going to live now," I said. "Remember? Remember we were here last week and we walked around and you said how much you liked the colors and that big giant painting in the dining room, the one of the ship out in the sea? And the nice ladies, the ladies playing Boggle in the dining room who said hi?"

She looked past me, as if trying to conjure one of those images in the distance—the painting, the Boggle-playing women—for clarity, for explanation of her current situation. But whatever she saw did not illuminate. She shook her head.

"This is where I'm going to live?"

"That's right," I confirmed.

"I don't think I like it. I don't think I like it at all."

We stood there for a while. What else was there to do? She glanced around the room, intense, silent, starting to understand. Her eyes turned back to me, her son, her only child. She had lost a lot of weight by then, was extremely weak, and I thought that she might fall to a heap at any moment. I imagined that I would have to catch her and how utterly weightless she would be in my arms. Her eyes continued to search mine for meaning; they were like two green open wounds.

When I returned home that afternoon, I walked through the empty house as if for the first time, surveying every room like I was a prospective homeowner.

But my life did not significantly change, not like I thought it would. For more than two years she's lived in the home and I've continued to live here. During that time my health has worsened while hers has actually improved. And now she's missing.

As I shave, swab deodorant, loosen my belt another discouraging notch, I try to picture where she might be: running (if that's even possible), crossing the highway, crouching by an extinguished campfire eating beans straight from the can. It's ridiculous, I know. But that's the movie trailer that plays in my head. She's talking to people, transients like herself. They huddle to keep warm. They tell stories because that's all they have now. One by one they speak. Then it's my mom's turn. She tells them her story. But all that doesn't matter now, she informs the crowd. I'm going to make it. For the first time in my life I'm truly free.

And they believe every word. Old bald women in bathrobes eating beans by a fire—well, they just don't lie.

Outside it's starting to rain, that perennial pissy mist that never fails to dampen my heart even though you'd think I'd be used to it by now. I go downstairs and into the living room to collect my thoughts. But there's distraction. The TV is on. And my roommate Raymond is there because he's always there.

"What do you mean missing?" he asks between bites of Nutter Butter, after I fill him in on the morning's revelations.

"Missing as in absence. As in the opposite of presence. The director says he's on it. They're on it. It's a stage something."

"Well if it was me I'd call the cops, pronto," advises a supremely confident, supremely stoned Raymond. "Fuck those amateurs at On Golden Pond. Call the cops. That's what I'd do," he says, sprawled on the sofa that's mine watching the TV that's also mine. "But hey, I'm just a take-charge Dirty Harry kinda guy. A man's got to know his limitations."

Raymond, who claims to be a successful seducer of the under-forty divorcées who frequent The Skinny Dip over in Falling Brook. I'm a freelance graphic artist, he tells them, and it's what he tells me. But ever since he's been living here he's never worked, not as far as I can tell, freelance or otherwise; he's always at home, either camped out in front of the TV or reading my magazines or smoking my pot. But he's reasonably quiet and clean and somehow pays his rent (I don't ask). Compared to some of the other roommates I've had since my mother entered A.A., Raymond qualifies as British royalty.

"Dirty Harry wouldn't call the cops," I say. "He'd go and take care of it himself."

"That's a good point," Raymond concedes. "I guess I didn't think that one through too well. Nutter Butter?"

Instead of calling the police I decide to drive over to the home. After that I'll take it from there. Who knows. She might already be back. She's creeping up on seventy, an old and frail woman who can't stand it when the temperature dips below eighty degrees. How long could she hold out?

As I'm gathering my keys and wallet and jacket, Raymond glances up from the consuming radius of the screen. It's either a game show or a talk show. People are laughing, applauding.

"I think we need some cereal," he says. "And juice." Then he adds, "If you happen to be going by a store, I mean."

The drive is mostly a straight shot, fifteen, twenty minutes tops, taking me from one side of the valley to the other. In between there's nothing but forgotten neighborhoods, occasional gas stations, the penitentiary-looking junior high school, a strip mall or two, vacant lots, dirt, mud. Along the way I try to ignore the gray funk massing steadily in the sky. Old Testament clouds are waiting ahead of me; the rain picks up. I click on my windshield wipers, wondering if my mother has been able to find cover, perhaps a barn or hunter's shack.

Whenever it rains long enough and hard enough, our inadequate town of Rayburn floods. Water rushes down from both sides into the valley, wreaking havoc on our homes and streets, reminding us of our vulnerabilities. Over the years various attempts have been made to stem the flow of the rain, but no matter what we do—improvised dams, rain gutters, more culverts, Native American healing rituals—the water seems to win. You're always hearing about a child or beloved family pet being washed away by an overflowing Jessup Creek. Little League season invariably gets scrapped, the Hound Dog Bar and Grill holds its annual flood party where beers are half-off and the jukebox is free. It's just something we put up with. Weather. What can you do?

I pass through Rayburn's equivalent of a downtown, a three-block cluster of economic woe. Most of the businesses have folded. Everyone goes elsewhere to shop, to see a movie, to eat out. Lately there's been talk of renovating the downtown area, of trying to lure in some chain stores. Our mayor, Larry, has even used the term "renaissance" and commissioned the community college's part-time art instructor to draw up the proposal. But we're all pretty doubtful. We've seen too much already. Too much hasn't happened for too long.

By the time I make it to the home the rain is pouring like hell, verging on the biblical. I sprint from the parking lot into the main building, getting drenched in the process. No one is around, the front desk unoccupied, so I shake off some more water and head down the hallway toward the dining area and first-floor rooms. A.A. always freaks me out. I feel like a traveler, crossing one country's border and entering another. Language, customs, currency—everything changes. Plus I usually get lost. It's like a large maze, full of fun-house wrong turns and stairways leading nowhere. Take a left instead of a right and you'll spend the next fifteen minutes finding your way back. Stop paying attention to where you're going and next thing you know you're in a room full of senior citizens singing "The Hokey-Pokey," or you come upon a hallway lined with people in wheelchairs and clutching walkers and you won't want to turn tail because they've already spotted you and it would be a huge snub, and so you keep walking, and as you do so they reach out to touch you and say something like "I don't belong here. There's been a terrible mistake."

Still walking and still I don't see anyone. Muzak drifts in through overhead speakers, barely audible but enough to annoy. I hear the clanking of cutlery and dishes, some ambient moaning. It's hard to believe that people live here, day to day. But before I get much farther a hand descends on my shoulder.

Turning, I behold a Sasquatch of a man. He's dressed in a yellow windbreaker, the kind security guards wear at rock concerts. His hair is buzzed and the hint of a goatee circles his unamused mouth. He's big. Insanely big. That's about all I can register. His bigness.

"I'm Michael Ormsby," I say. "My mother lives here. Muriel Ormsby. I was told she's missing."

"Missing?" the man repeats, his meaty paw of a hand still vise-gripped on my shoulder. "Jesus, not another one. What's with these damn fucking old people?"

I'm escorted back to the entry area. Now there's a woman at the front desk, hunched over a computer keyboard like a mad scientist, tapping furiously. Rows and rows of bricks fill the expanse of the screen. Tetris.

"I'm listening," she says without removing her eyes from the monitor.

"We got another runner," reports the windbreaker man.

"Name?"

The windbreaker man turns to me.

"Ormsby," I say. "Muriel Ormsby. The director called me this morning."

"There's no reason to shout, sir," snaps the Tetris woman. "Violence and intimidation will get you nowhere in this facility."

I hadn't shouted at all. Hadn't been violent. Hadn't intimidated. I was beginning to regret the half-assed research I did about this place. It was nearby. It was convenient. It was cheap. Well, cheaper.

"I'm just trying to find out what's going on with my mother," I say. "That's all. She's a client here."

"Just a—shit." And she thwacks the keyboard in disgust. "Stupid addictive game," she tells the screen. "So your mother has gone missing. Ormsby. I think I saw a memo earlier today. Or was it yesterday? Yeah. Ormsby. Actually I think there's a posse getting ready to head out pretty soon. You probably can still catch them."

"A posse?"

"Just a couple of local fellas who do a little freelance work for us when it comes to client searches. They're real good about it. They get sensitivity training and everything."

"And the director. Could I see him first?"

She laughs. "I don't think so. I suggest talking to Carl and Dale. They're the posse guys. Malcolm here, he can show you the way."

Malcolm extends a Schwarzenegger forearm to show me the way. I'm about to thank the Tetris woman, but this time I catch myself. How could I have put my mother in a place like this? Where is she? How far has she gone by now? Has she hitched? Jumped a train? Twisted an ankle? Fallen and can't get up? It's several miles into town. After that there's nothing but forest and mountains and the army base; after that, the Pacific Ocean. I'm starting to hope that she makes it to wherever it is she thinks she's going, that she stays disappeared.

With the exception of my three and a half years of college, I've lived in Rayburn all my life. Why? It's a good question. Prospects here—economic, spiritual, you name it—are few and far between. The town itself isn't small enough to be intimate and charming, but neither is it big enough to offer any cosmopolitan amenities. Most of the women close to my age are either unavailable or have sworn off the habit of men forever. And the rain—we're always wet, drizzled on, sun-deprived. But after a certain point in life, you just get used to a place, how it's laid out, how it looks, how it feels. It's what you know. It's where you live. You've made your choice even though it doesn't really feel like one, and there's no specific moment you made that decision, it just happened, and now there are too many miles and too many years between you and that moment that never happened.

•

We find Carl and Dale in the parking lot, warming up their pickup truck and drinking 7-Eleven coffee. They wear camouflage fatigues, green rain ponchos, baseball caps that advertise the manufacturers of large farm equipment. You could mistake them for twins except that one sports a prodigious beard and one does not. Both are burly, thick, men of one-syllable pleasures. Malcolm approaches the truck and tells them who I am.

"Want to tag along, chief?" one of them says. "We're heading out to Timmins Ranch. We got a report of a confused elderly white female roaming the area. Would that there description fit your mother?"

"Generally, yes."

"Well hop in then, captain."

I scrunch into the back portion of the cab, totally soaked. Introductions are made. Carl is the driver. Dale, the one who's been speaking and has the beard, shakes my hand, crushes it actually. It's then, while waiting for the circulation to return to my white-collar fingers, that I notice the rifles.

"So Mike. What is it you do in the real world?" Dale asks.

I hesitate. I feel like my answer is being recorded, will be scrutinized, judged. I regret—and not for the first time—my particular career path. "I'm a payroll clerk over at Jackson General."

Dale purses his mouth some, as if considering whether or not this fit his criteria for a respectable profession.

"Carl's been there."

Carl nods as he pulls onto the main highway. His hands on the steering wheel look raw, capable of sudden violence. Three guns. Rifles. With those scope things you look through. One two three.

"Damn near killed himself a few years back," Dale continues. "Done got caught under a mudslide. But Carl made it out. Survived. His dog didn't, though."

"That was a damn fine specimen of dog," says Carl. "Only wished I'd breeded him."

We drive in silence for a while, until they resume a conversation they'd been having earlier. Carl mentions that his wife's sister's roommate is pregnant. Again. There's some question about the identity and race of the father. All the while I keep trying to come up with various ways to casually inquire about the guns. Finally, Dale realizes what's making me so uneasy.

"What, those things? Don't worry none. There's no real bullets. These are just tranquilizers. Like what vets and nature people use and stuff. It'll knock you out. But it won't kill you, not hardly."

"So you shoot them? You actually shoot the people you're looking for?"

"Like I said, tranquilizer. They get hit, they go to sleep, they wake up back at A.A., good as new."

"And you do this regularly?"

"Say again there, Mike."

"Work for the home. Track down people who've left."

"It's—what you call it? A fluctuating market, like anything else. Carl and I, we have a couple of different business ventures in the works. Diversify. That's our motto. Today's entrepreneur can't limit himself to just one deal. Think different, think out of the box, synergy and all that. But the work's been pretty steady as of late. We were just talking yesterday about how we need another person. An apprentice like. You interested in switching careers, Mike? Left, Carl, left."

The truck veers off the highway onto an unpaved road. There's a barn to our left, crops of some kind on our right. Everything is green and wet. "We'll just wait and see how you do," says Dale. "How's that sound? A little on-the-job training."

Carl brings the truck to a stop in a clearing and cuts the engine. Hanging from the rearview mirror is a pair of handcuffs. Empty cigarette packs and crumpled fast-food bags litter the dashboard. I can see their breath inside the cab, steady gusts escaping then disappearing. Dale hands me a rifle.

"Lock and load," he says.

It's Sunday. Day of rest. Day of atonement. Day of football and naps and *The Simpsons*. Tomorrow I'll be back at work, at my desk, poorly postured as I type numbers into a computer. Then I'll come home and

Raymond will be there, eyes aglaze with TV and weed, nursing a Zima and quoting lines from *The Big Lebowski*, regaling me with factoids about James Polk's sexual appetites and recent outbreaks of whooping cough, providing a blow-by-blow account of the bidding battle for an obscure toy or game from his childhood that he found on eBay. But for now I'm following Dale and Carl, the rain thrumming down, and we're hunting my mother.

They move quickly—faster than you'd think, based on their bodies and ample bellies—and I have a tough time keeping up. Visibility is pretty minimal because of the rain, but Dale and Carl forge ahead, as if they know exactly where they're going, men of the wild, suckled by wolves. We enter a heavily forested patch where hardly any rain falls. Pine soaks the air, along with the damp of leaves and earth. I chase after their green shapes as best I can. The asthma: it snakes around my lungs then squeezes like a motherfucker. "Through here," Dale yells, motioning for me to hurry.

At the top of a small ridge Carl scans the area below with his high-tech-looking binoculars. "This is where we found one of them last week," he says, handing the binoculars to Dale. "They usually follow the highway then turn up that road we took. Once they get past the farm there ain't much elsewhere they can go, see, just straight into this big meadow which is where we're going. Like shooting ducks in a bathtub. The only trouble is, is when some of the more stubborn ones wander over onto the army base, what with all the exercises and maneuvers and such they're always doing. We've had a few ugly situations there. You say this is your mother?"

"I don't know. It could be her. All I know is she's been reported missing."

"There's been a lot of that lately," Dale says. "That's where Carl here comes in handy. He's kind of psychic on these matters."

Carl produces a sock from inside his poncho. He holds it up for my inspection. "This your mother's sock?" It's a white sock gone gray, washed too many times. I can't identify it as my mother's. It's a sock.

"Carl takes an object of the person who's missing—say a sock, a shirt, a purse, a used wad of Kleenex—and he can sense where the person is," Dale explains. "You probably seen this kind of stuff on *Dateline* or *20/20*. Carl here's got a gift."

"And I've got a real bead on this sock," says Carl, sounding almost wistful. "I'm thinking that way." He points north. Or is it south? The rain lets up momentarily. Dale shakes his head, says, "It won't hold. The rain's gonna get worse before it gets better. Let's keep a moving." They take off down a narrow trail, graceful as elk in a PBS documentary, and soon I'm once again huffing horribly like a repentant smoker.

The Tetris woman had said freelance. So did Carl and Dale get paid on a per-person basis? And whose policy was this? The director's? Shooting residents, hunting them like animals? Certainly this wasn't legal. Certainly I could complain to the proper authorities. I began to compose police blotter sketches of Dale and Carl as well as Malcolm and the Tetris woman. Arrests were no doubt imminent. Until then, however, I'd have to remain calm, act cordial, let things play out.

"Mike. Over here."

My rifle grows heavier. Have I ever fired a gun? No, I have not. I slog through some more foliage, through more mud and muck, and emerge into another clearing. Sure, there is a slight elation, the euphoria of the predator. But I keep having to remind myself: this is my mother, the woman who gave birth to me, not a deer or quail. Mud covers my shoes and most of my pants. My jacket is now just an extra layer of wet. I squint ahead and see Carl pointing like a Civil War general. Down below us, moving at a labored pace, as if blind, is a woman, obviously old, obviously confused. "I knew that sock was powerful," Carl says.

Dale clasps his comrade's shoulder. "Bingo. There's our runner. That her?" he asks me.

At first I can't be certain. The woman is too far away. But slowly she comes into focus and I'm pretty sure it's my mother. It's been years since I've seen her without a wig, but yes, it's her. I recognize the hobbled body, the osteoporosis lurch, the powder-blue terry cloth robe I gave her years ago.

"Carl, I believe this one's yours," says Dale.

Carl smiles like a villain in a James Bond movie, drawing the rifle up to his eye. I expect him to speak with an unidentifiable accent.

"Just a second and I'll have a pretty clear shot. Come on. Come on you bitch. Keep moving."

"Hey," says Dale. "That's his mother you're talking about."

"Sorry there, skipper," Carl apologizes. "Nothing personal."

The woman, my mother, is the most fragile creature I've ever seen. From up here, she's so alone, so small, not at all the person I grew up with. She's just a sad, lonely, old woman who shouldn't be out in the rain and lost and scared and making a run for it. I see my failure.

Carl continues to peer through the scope thing, anticipating. Dale pulls out a cigarette and smokes in the rain.

And I don't know precisely why or how, but just in time I'm possessed by some kind of recessive heroic gene finally come to life and my arms start moving and then I'm running and charging like a blitzing linebacker and I grab the snout of Carl's gun as he's pulling the trigger and the shot falls short, way short. There's immediate wrestling, pounding, I'm on the ground, knees in my chest, boot heels in my stomach. I taste bark, blood. Carl and Dale roll me over and pin my arms behind my back. Breathing isn't an option. I'm completely covered in mud and ooze, practically primordial. "What the shit boy?" They drag me to my feet. Standing requires all my remaining energy. "Hold him." Carl grabs my throat, weighing the possibilities.

Amazing: one action, one desperate and foolish move—and this is what happens. Things change. Or could change. The outcome possibly altered. So sudden. That simple.

"You're one big fucking inconvenience, Mr. Payroll Clerk," says Dale.

But I have no illusions, not even in my fuzzy state. I know it's only temporary, that sooner or later they'll bring my mother back to Arcadian Acres and that she'll resume her life of solitude and I'll return to my equally ascetic existence. But even if it got her only a few minutes more, then it was worth it. To have that much more freedom. It's the only gift I can give her. Maybe she's somewhere else in her mind and this will allow her to stay there a little longer. Maybe she's reliving her childhood at this very moment. Maybe she's remembering what it was like to be a young girl with no idea of what lay ahead, no conception of towns like Rayburn and nursing homes and disappointing husbands and distant sons.

The blood surges in my head. It's like a blender in there, puréeing like mad. I won't be vertical for much longer, this I know. My legs weakening, gravity saying fuck it, too bad. Dale lifts his rifle, tossing the cigarette and stabbing it out with his boot. I want to yell *run*, to warn her of the piercing tranquilizer about to enter her body and put an end to her doomed journey. But it's impossible to speak with Carl's fingers locked around my throat. He smiles because he hadn't expected such drama today. But this time there won't be any last-minute heroics. Still, I've done something, no matter how stupid or small. As my body gives way (it happens in slow-mo, and it's not at all unwelcome) I feel satisfied for the first time since I don't know when. The last thing I see before everything goes black is a lone figure streaking across the soggy landscape below, slow but steady, a cautious body finding its way in the world.

I wake up in my mother's room, slumped in a chair, body aching and waterlogged, throat sore and scratchy from my adventure with Carl and Dale. She's in bed, asleep, and I just listen and watch her; mouth open, the restless intake of air, the geriatric wheeze, the weak rise of her chest. It's the most time we've spent together in ages. I watch and watch for I don't know how long, realizing that there is another gift I can give her.

There: a phone on the dresser by the bed. The phone I never called her on. It works.

"Raymond, hey, it's me, Michael," I say. "Yeah. Look. There's no real way to work up to this, so, but something has come up and you're going to have to move out."

I explain that my mother will be coming back home, that it's just one of those things, nothing personal, life happens the way it happens. But he must be high, immersed in rerun bliss, because all he says is "Cool, that's cool," probably not understanding that he'll soon have to vacate the house and answer classified ads and start leeching off someone else.

"And if you do go by a store on the way back, could you get some tortillas and cheese, too?" asks Raymond.

Again, I watch my mother sleep. The deep, branching lines in her face and forehead and neck seem to go on and on, evidence, the nameless markings of a life. She's still unwigged. The last few remaining patches of thin white hair cling to her scalp. A blanket hides the rest of her body, and it's easy to imagine someone—a coroner, a priest— pulling it up over her face and pronouncing her dead. But she's not. She's breathing, albeit slowly. I wonder if she's cold, if she could use another blanket. But I don't want to wake her up. She needs sleep. She needs time. She needs a son who can be a son.

Maybe we'll pick up where we left off. Maybe it will be different. Either way, it will be better for her than being here. And either way, I'll be changing her diaper and crushing up the pills that are too big for her to swallow whole, dissolving the powder in applesauce or pudding, ministering as best I can, hiring someone to take care of her while I'm at work. But I'm trying not to worry about the details. Not now. Not yet.

Later on, just as it's starting to turn dark, the long day finally conceding to night, someone enters the room. Doesn't knock. Just walks right in. A man.

"Mr. Ormsby," he whispers. "I'm Dr. Daniel Todd, the director. I see you're awake."

And I know there will be explanations, forms to fill out, the red tape to be sifted through and fussed over and finalized, but for now a simple declaration will do: Yes, I'm awake.

THE BOYFRIEND

THE BOYFRIEND

THE BOYFRIEND KNOWS HE should say something. It's the proper time, the right amount of silence has uncomfortably elapsed, and if he doesn't utter some kind of solace or at the very least resort to a well-traveled cliché pretty soon here, she will start to wonder what's going on and why he isn't reciprocating, isn't responding to her immediate needs, which are really quite simple: for him to say something, anything, although ideally something reassuring and supportive of her place in the world as a human being of import and snowflake uniqueness. And he should be saying something along those lines, he should be responding and reciprocating and so on. It shouldn't be so difficult. He knows this. It's the time-honored boyfriendly thing to do, he's fully aware, and plus he's been the boyfriend for a long enough period of time that he should be able to read her many female moods and nuances and signs (some subtle, some not so subtle, as was the case with her exclamation, only seconds ago, of "My life is fuck-fucking shit") and thus intuit what is, what could be, the right thing to say. At least get a ballpark sense. Only he cannot. He cannot summon the necessary language that will end this swelling stalemate and make everything all right so that she will then continue on with her crying and confessing and whatever else requires release, knowing that if nothing else he has acknowledged her pain in the obligatory boyfriend way, accepted it, perhaps even understood it a little, maybe. Instead, as he holds her, growing impatient in spite of himself, smelling her unwashed hair, his mind races with all kinds of weird, unrelated stuff that boyfriends most definitely should not be thinking of at a time like this (like how her hair smells unwashed, and who but him is dumb enough to talk smack to a cop after you've already had two DUIs this year, and what's up with all those celebrities who are into Scientology?), and just now he detects the slightest, smallest hint of nipple blooming underneath her blouse, but there it is, what can he do—not notice? As a boyfriend, he knows that such A.D.D. insensitivity could be considered a major liability in the eyes of most girlfriends, including his. He reasons, however, that he is the boyfriend and not the husband, not the father, and that there is a significant distinction here. This helps calm him. This differentiation— between the words "boyfriend" and, on the other hand, "husband" and "father"—this, he gratifyingly realizes, makes a huge big fucking difference. Just the boyfriend. The freedom that that allows. Which is after all part of the attraction, the lure, of being the boyfriend and nothing more. Truth is, he doesn't see how he'll ever reach the point where he can be anything but that, the boyfriend, but who knows, he is young, life bitch-slaps you around in ways you never expect or see coming (his cousin in Florida, for instance, who one day was making good money at UPS and the next was on disability and eating all his meals through a tube), and too there's the fact that he has some friends—disturbingly increasing in number come to think of it—who have graduated from boyfriends to husbands and/or fathers, although they do not talk too much about this transformation, which he's pretty sure is a few years away for him personally, if ever, but then again you never know, as the example of his cousin in Florida illustrates. Really, who knows anything. Like for instance: she might be pregnant and that might be the real reason why she is crying—not because some S.S. supervisor at work embarrassed her in front of everyone and spurred a self-confidence crisis, but because she has not been able to bring herself to tell him of the pregnancy because he is not husband/father material let alone boyfriend material—and soon, very soon, his life will dramatically change and he doesn't even know it yet, like a dope he's been going to his job and working out at the gym and renting movies he's already seen like three times while this unspoken fate awaits him, and it has all narrowed down to this moment, sitting here, present tense, on the itchy sofa he's always hated (in his defense, hardly a conducive setting for cuddling and intimacy) with her head still buried in his chest and he's stroking her hair but it's just not the same as saying something to console her, for which it's too late now anyway. I'm just a boyfriend, he tries to reassure himself, only it doesn't work as well as it did a few seconds ago. She stirs a little, pulls away some. And that small retreat contains multitudes. And he knows she's not pregnant, that's not it. No, it's what he initially suspected, simply that there's been the escalation he'd dreaded, only now it's official, verified: the situation at hand is no longer merely about her self-confidence crisis but also now involves the issue of his response, his lack of response, his silence, his guilt, his inadequacy—not only his own, which was considerable, but his entire gender's, maybe. It's not the first time this has come up, with this particular girlfriend in addition to others in the past. Not surprisingly, the boyfriend's track record as a boyfriend has not been good, not good at all, but the girlfriend, it should probably be pointed out, knew this going into the relationship, which has had its ups and downs, but no more or less than usual.

MEXICO

MEXICO

LATER THEY WOULD DIVORCE and there would be much bitterness and friends wound up choosing sides (his fault, her fault, etc.) and the question of who was deserving of the elaborate home entertainment system would never be resolved in a satisfactory manner, but when they left for Mexico they were still very much in love and generally hopeful about the future. And like just about everyone else, they were not able to foresee, let alone imagine, the changes looming invisibly, inevitably ahead. One day life was one way, the next it was another. You wake up in a different bed in a different city with a different person beside you. How did I get here? Am I the same person I was when I was with person A and not person B (or C, or D), who's mumbling in his/her sleep as if trying to verbalize something important, a warning of some kind perhaps? And before too long it's hard to conjure the existence that preceded the current one. Photographs help but only a little, mainly for remembering dates and trips and hairstyles; they are purely for documentation purposes; they tell you nothing more than I was there and now I am here.

The flight from Los Angeles to Mexico City was long and draining, a dreaded red eye, which made them pledge (mutually, right after the captain finished his bilingual announcements about the approximate arrival time) to forever avoid late-night air travel, no matter the savings involved. Most of the other passengers were Mexicans. More specifically: Mexican men. Many had large cardboard boxes that they lugged on the plane and expertly squeezed into the overhead bins, and many wore straw cowboy hats and duct-taped cowboy boots. He complained about the legroom. She complained about a migraine that had successfully deployed while she purchased Gas-X and a copy of *Elle* at the airport gift shop. Around two-thirty in the morning they were fed enchiladas puddled in red sauce and then they tried to sleep. They went through customs in Guadalajara, getting off the plane and then getting back on, an Olympian and seemingly unnecessary procedure that left them even more depleted and crabby. Once in Mexico City they hailed a taxi, a kamikaze green-and-yellow VW bug with the passenger seat removed, an area where they were instructed to put their luggage (and, after doing so and simultaneously noting the lack of seatbelts with a look of coded American disapproval, how could they not picture themselves—him, that is, since she was sitting behind the driver who would presumably act as a buffer—flying through the windshield and ending this vacation before it even began). The car sharked its way in and out of the taxi-heavy traffic—and along the way they got a small but that's-enough-for-me-thanks glimpse of the metropolis' infamous sprawl and spewing pollution and brown-clotted sky—eventually delivering them to one of the city's many bus stations where they bought two tickets for Oaxaca, six or so hours to the south. The tickets were cheap even though the bus was considered first class. Which meant, they soon discovered, that it had air conditioning and multiple TVs mounted from the ceiling, all down the aisle. During the course of the trip, three Steven Seagal movies were played back to back. You could see his hairline receding further and further with each film. At one point she woke up amid the explosions and poor marksmanship of the vaguely Middle Eastern terrorists and said, "Isn't it over yet?" And he said: "It's a different one, go back to sleep." And then he watched her sleep, his wife, his beautiful sleeping wife, and stared out at a landscape that struck him as barren, ugly, hard. Mexico had been her idea.

By the time they arrived at their hotel in Oaxaca (it was only recently that he learned it was pronounced *Wa-Ha-ka* and not *O-x-ah-ka*) he had been up for well over twenty-four hours and she had slept only intermittently on the bus ride/Seagal film festival. They collapsed on the bed like a couple of defeated triathletes. The room overlooked a courtyard from which they could hear the delicate tinkling of a fountain. They were too tired to make love but they did so anyway. Quicker than usual but extremely satisfying nonetheless. The brevity—what? Compacting the pleasure maybe, making each groan and give more potent, more vital. They slept for fourteen hours straight.

The next day they didn't get started until late morning, still travel weary and mildly disoriented and consulting their mini library of travel books. They showered, considered making love again (but didn't), applied their SPF 50 sunscreen, packed up the backpack, and set off to explore the town. Today would be an orientation/recovery day. Tomorrow there would be a trip to some nearby ruins and an indigenous village. The day after that renting ATVs. Then another marathon bus ride to the coast, to Puerto Angel, where they'd spend a week in deep relaxation mode before flying back to Mexico City and then home.

The Zócalo—lined with restaurants and cafés and trinket shops as well as people asking the Corona-sipping tourists for money—was only a few blocks from the hotel. They passed the woman twice. She was sitting on the sidewalk, barefoot, a package of some kind in her lap, sporadically talking to herself and/or the package. She wore what seemed to be layers of brightly colored skirts and a black Florida Marlins T-shirt with the sleeves cut off. Young, but probably not as young as you'd initially think. Rocking like a little girl who's lost and about to cry. Just baking away in the sun, oblivious to the heat. It was on the third time that she stood up and ghost-shuffled up to them and tried to hand over the package, Spanish slowly hissing out of her mouth, too late for them to escape.

"I don't understand. What? No," she said. "I don't want it. *No gracias. No gracias por favor.* Whatever it is, I'm sorry, no. What's she saying?"

They walked faster, but the woman followed.

"You don't want to know," he said, able to translate most of the woman's ramblings, having minored in Spanish to complement his international business degree.

"What's she saying? Tell me."

"She's saying it's a baby."

"What's a baby?"

"The package, what she's holding and trying to give us. And she's saying she wants to sell it to us, the baby. It's for sale. She's saying—I think it's what she's saying—that we, we'll give it a better life. The United States is a very beautiful place. She's saying if we don't buy it she's going to just leave it out on the...Uh, I'm having a little trouble following the rest."

"*Muerte,*" the woman proclaimed, continuing to shadow, bowing her head repeatedly, extending the package toward them like it was a sacrifice to the gods. People were looking now: other tourists, the locals, the street vendors. It was becoming a scene.

"What's that? Muh-where-tay? I think I know what that means. What's she saying now?"

"Nothing," he said. "Let's just keep moving. There. That store. Let's go inside. She won't come in."

"But what's she saying?"

"You don't want to know."

"I do want to know."

"You're not going to like it."

"Tell me."

He realized then that he could tell her the truth or lie. Somehow her insistence helped him choose the former.

"Okay," he began. "She's saying something like—I don't know—like the baby will die if we don't buy it."

"She said what?"

"Sweetie, never mind. It's just a ploy. She probably says the same thing to every American who walks by. And it's probably not even a real baby in there."

But just as he spoke that last sentence, as if the woman understood the meaning of his privileged *norteamericano* words (and perhaps she did), she jumped out in front of them so they had to stop. The woman then tore away part of the package's wrapping and underneath they could clearly see it: a small, small baby, very real and very red, and puffy, crowned with a dark thatch of thin hair, a language-less gurgle of new, uncertain life, fingers futilely probing, eyes still pinched shut and not yet ready to view the world. They maneuvered around the woman, started walking again.

"Just don't look back," he said.

"I'm not, I won't," she said. But she did.

Finally, suddenly, the woman gave up. She circled back to her spot on the sidewalk, covered up the baby, resumed her rocking, and just like that it was over. The sun was bursting at full capacity now, situated directly over the Zócalo and filling the sky with a fierce whiteness. They were thirsty. And hungry. After scrutinizing several menus they settled on a restaurant that was upstairs, called Casa Amigo. She was practically shaking. She couldn't stop thinking about it: the woman, the baby, the Spanish words ringing in her head. He was already starting to forget the incident, one of those weird random things that sort of freak you out at the time but quickly fade away. She wanted to call the police, report it to the proper authorities. He wanted a margarita like you wouldn't believe.

The woman was there in the same spot the next day as well. Without the package. The package was gone. She smiled (an evil smile, a witch's smile) as they walked past and pretended not to notice her (but did).

The ruins were ruins, the indigenous village a tourist trap. The ATVs couldn't get over twenty-five and kept breaking down. The hotel in Puerto Angel was nice but not as nice as the website made it seem. There were mild sunburns but thankfully no major stomach flare-ups, despite a close call with some ceviche. (They made sure to avoid ice and salads—that's where most people slip up, paying for it dearly.) They took naps, lounged on the beach, saying little to each other. The trip had been tainted, haunted. At least for her. She flashed forward and saw them looking at their photo album with a group of friends and only being able to think of the woman and the package and how he would shush her if she started to talk about it, which she probably wouldn't anyway because it's so damn depressing and why spoil the evening but still. The baby was probably no more than a few days old. It looked so new, so raw, so utterly fragile and in need of bodily warmth, the simple truth of skin touching skin, a mother's heart beating nearby. She dreamed of the woman: her face, her murky eyes, her mouth jammed full of unruly teeth. That smile. Sometimes in the dreams the baby was her baby. And she turned away from it. She continued walking with her husband. Then, too, she dreamed of going back to the Zócalo and rescuing the child, tracking it down, bringing it back to their townhouse in Santa Monica, raising it as their own and giving it a life it never would have had, an act of redemption that changes everything. Whenever she returned to the subject (pretty much every few hours) he huffed and puffed. He didn't want to hear about it anymore. It was becoming something more than what it was: an aberration, a travel anecdote, a sad story that didn't have anything to do with them. "Christ, just let it go," he said. And she said: "I can't, I just can't." And he said, finally, on the last night of the trip, after one Corona too many: "I don't fucking get it with you sometimes."

When they got home the red light on their answering machine was blinking and beeping furiously, accusatorily, sixteen messages waiting, but they couldn't bring themselves to listen to them until the next day. It was Sunday. Fortunately they'd had the foresight to take that Monday off as well. They went food shopping, did laundry, returned calls. They made dinner reservations for their anniversary the following month. Three years. The marriage itself would last almost another two. One of the lawyers made the predictable comment about how much easier these things are when there are no children involved.

No, of course, they did not get divorced because a woman had tried to sell them a baby in Oaxaca. It was much, much more complicated than that. There were larger issues, severings that had been there but further developed and intensified over the subsequent months and years. For instance, their clashing and ultimately incompatible views of the universe: he a cynic, she only pretending to be a cynic; he a believer in free will and the power of the individual, she sensing that maybe forces beyond our control shape our lives in ways we can't fully fathom; he questioning the whole idea of parenthood, she finding herself lingering way too long at Baby Gap. Or the more mundane: he a fan of classic rock, she a devotee of Madonna and Brit pop; he a Mac person, she a PC person. Or the more erotic: he unwilling to do certain things sexually, she very willing to do certain things sexually. If each marriage is a mystery to the outside world, then perhaps there's a little bit of that with the participants, too.

But what was it, then, about the incident in the Zócalo? Had the event itself caused the fissure between them? Did it merely symbolize something else, shining a light on more substantial concerns? Had its narrative revealed traits and flaws that had previously been hidden or at least somewhat masked (his insularity and lack of compassion, her obsessing over seemingly unimportant matters, big picture-wise)? Did it somehow amplify discord and dissatisfaction that was already there, gestating, that had been steadily insinuating itself into their lives but they were only just now noticing? Or was it merely an isolated occurrence that signified nothing whatsoever? Both had their suspicions, which never amounted to more than that—speculations, late-night ruminations, Chardonnay-fueled hypotheses that lost their relevance by morning. Yet no matter the exact meaning of the event, it did, however, signal a shift. It was a beginning, a turning.

Now when friends or associates or prospective lovers ask her why the marriage didn't work out (it comes up sooner or later), she says because a woman tried to sell her a baby in Mexico. Then she laughs, enjoying her own personal little joke that no one else could possibly get (she thinks it's funny, witty, enigmatic), and goes on to somberly recite some of the real reasons, that is if the listener hasn't been too put off by her esoteric opening line. And when friends or associates or prospective lovers ask him why the marriage didn't work out (it comes up sooner or later as well), he plays it safe and says it was that old familiar story: two people who loved each other but just not enough.

BURN

BURN

IT WASN'T EVEN TEN a.m. and already the day had consequences. Why? Because not long after settling in for the morning at her designated workstation, her second cup of coffee not yet fully registering, and right after the computer guy failed (again) to fix the phantom problem with the order-taking software that had been driving her nuts for the past two weeks, DataCorp Transaction Processing Specialist Ramona Dupree had fucked up and agreed to go out on a date with her Level B Supervisor, Victor Nance, a guy who, sure, seemed kind of sweet in that I'm-thirty-eight-and-still-live-at-home-and-collect-Civil-War-memorabilia sort of way but who also creepily verged on the Lee Harvey Oswaldish. Even more than that, though, he was her boss, and such intimacies often ended in disaster, as Ramona could unfortunately testify from firsthand experience. Plus, too, he wasn't her type; he was her antitype. He used words like "swell" and "guesstimate" on a regular basis, incorporating way too frequent Star Wars and Star Trek references into his training speeches and general conversation.

As soon as she said yes she regretted it. Somehow her tongue had been temporarily hijacked. Victor had caught her off guard, snuck up from behind as she was typing, typing away, and then blindsided her. She wanted to take that simple word, *yes* (an affirmation that would end in ruin), and exchange it for another one, its exact opposite in fact: *no*. But it was too late. It was always too late.

"Shall we say…next Thursday, then?"

Victor was still standing behind her. She hadn't even turned around or swiveled her swivel chair, although she could smell his Listerine cloud and see the reflection of his smiling little-boy face in her monitor.

"Okay, great," he confirmed. "Thursday it is. And I'm gonna hold you to that."

And before she could snap out of it and summon the necessary verbal skills that would prevent this small mistake from spiraling into a much larger one, Victor was gone, power-walking off to another terminal, cheerfully assisting a new trainee in the fine art of handling charge-backs. Ramona resumed her work. She tried to concentrate. She tried not to think of the boys. She hammered at the keyboard as if the letters and numbers and commands would yield some kind of understanding if she only hit them hard enough, long enough. But they didn't. They let her down, and her fingers grew sore, and she had to withdraw to a bathroom stall for a good ten minutes, the longest you could be away from your workstation without arousing suspicion.

Later it was Alexis, an assistant something to somebody in Payroll, who caused Ramona's stomach to tighten an additional knot, it being news that there were any knots left. She, Alexis, with her Mrs. Brady hair and stuffed animals and framed pictures of her airbrushed, store-bought kids all over her cube, blew her, Ramona, some attitude because she had replaced the toner in the printer too early: "That one, dear, was still good for another fifty, sixty pages; you just need to take it out and give it a little bitty shake is all," Alexis sermoned, as if speaking to a potty-mouthed preschooler.

And then someone else, probably the office ho Yolanda from Human Resources/Internal Development, spoiled her lunch by pinching her fruit-on-the-bottom yogurt (boysenberry, nonfat) from the fridge, a successful heist even though Ramona had strategically positioned the plastic cup behind several Chinese takeout cartons and a Styrofoam container that had been abandoned for weeks. It was a setback that forced her to deal with the notoriously unreliable vending machine, and sure enough, seventy-five cents later she was left with nothing but a dangling SnackWells Crème Sandwich that despite her emphatic shoves and improvised karate kicks could not be dislodged from its B5 slot.

And then finally—finally after a relatively uneventful afternoon (computer crashing, a chatty customer who didn't mind sharing her numerous ailments and details about her ungrateful daughters) and just as she was about to leave for the day, having endured another shift and avoided any further contact with her boss, Victor spotted her passing the supply room. He had this totally clichéd and pathetic puppy dog look, as though there was a sappy heavy rotation lite-rock love song playing in his head, which there probably was. Eye contact had been made, so she couldn't ignore him. Ramona waved, trying to make sure the gesture would be interpreted as neutral, not too encouraging, just part of the common human experience: waving good-bye to a coworker at the end of another long day. But Victor was beyond the time-space continuum thing. He beamed.

So it wasn't all that surprising, really, that her patience and overall capacity to absorb life's little unforeseen twists and turns already had diminished significantly by the time she was on the freeway headed home, the evening ahead beholding nothing but the promise of dishes, *Home Improvement* reruns, and the obligatory weekly phone call to her born-again sister in St. Louis. The commute was a crawl. All the way thinking, worrying: Something was coming. She could feel it, feel it deeply, like an ache in her bones, a whisper that becomes a roar. It could happen today or tomorrow or next week. It could be a car swerving into her lane or the boys getting into trouble at school. It could be health related: carpal tunnel or, worse, a terminal disease that nobody has ever heard of because it lacks a celebrity spokesperson. Or maybe one of the mystery illnesses the chatty customer had described, the one where different parts of your body go numb and they don't know why and there's nothing you can do about it. Whatever the specifics of the calamity, it would somehow find her. It was approaching, gathering momentum. It was only a matter of time, of circumstances once again conspiring against her. This was her life. This was the way the world worked.

Like always, Ramona parked her car in her assigned space, 143, a number that marked her and saddened her on a nightly basis; and like always, she took her time—why hurry?—traversing the large, potholed apartment building parking lot, which also happened to be the view from her second-floor bedroom window, the noise depriving her of countless hours of cherished sleep and the proximity providing her with an intimate knowledge of the comings and goings of the complex's anonymous teenagers who went there to urinate and take drugs and the like. Inside she was immediately greeted by the familiar howl of the TV, but the living room was suspiciously empty. She shed her keys and purse and the mail she wouldn't open. Then she heard the commotion. Smelled something.

"What's going on in there? What's burning?" she mildly yelled toward the kitchen, thinking Jiffy Pop, cookies, microwaved Play-Doh, boys will be boys, etc.

When she got no response, she went into the kitchen to investigate. And there he was, Sean Casey, her six year old, burning. Well not so much burning as emitting tiny puffs of smoke. The boy writhed and cried and rolled on the tiled kitchen floor as his older brother Kyle and Kyle's satanic friend Cole laughed like fairy tale trolls. They were trying to pin down the squirming Sean Casey, trying to light him again with an uncooperative Bic.

A barely audible "Oh my God" was all she could muster before pushing the boys away and pulling down some kitchen towels, wetting them, and then smothering her youngest son. She cradled him in her arms, crying herself now. She was afraid to look at him, but when she did she saw that it wasn't that bad. She'd made it just in time. The flames hadn't been able to take root. There was no visible damage to his skin or face. Just some redness and maybe a little irritation. He had several blackened marks on his T-shirt and pants, both unsalvageable, but that's all. Thank Jesus or Allah or whoever. She was relieved, sprawled out there on the floor with Sean Casey breathing heavily in her arms, but it didn't last for long.

These were her boys, her babies. She had used to sing to them at night, bewitch them to sleep. *Freight train, freight train, going so fast.* An old folk song that was their favorite. They had climbed into bed with her in the mornings and sometimes she let them stay. How had they gotten so far away from that? She wasn't ever in the present moment, it seemed, couldn't just be with her kids and not worry about what was next, what needed to be done, what pressing bullshit thing required fixing. Her mind, her thoughts forever racing forward. She turned out to be an even worse parent than she imagined. Nine times out of ten she would be patient, patient, patient, but then that tenth time she would slip, explode, release. The power struggles were constant: refusing to brush their teeth, tie their shoes, put their dishes away. Defiance was their default state. They both had hit her, hard, punched her in the stomach more than once, right where the scar from her C-section was. She grew angrier at them because they were in control and they knew it and she knew it and she wasn't able to do anything to change the situation. This fundamental failing as an adult, as a parent.

The anger now came quick, in one breaking burst. It was all so typical. Always some surprise, some epic mischief that seemed created just for her. To piss her off. To make her question everything.

"Why are you always doing this?" she said. "Why are you always doing this to me? What the hell is wrong with you two?"

Life is a cabernet. That was the message of a license plate holder that she'd seen recently, and that had prompted Ramona to seriously consider ramming the shit out of the Secret Service-black Lexus that sported it. But life was no cabernet for her. It wasn't even a bottle of Boone's Farm, what with the kids, the bad jobs, the bad men, the bad decisions. The whole predictable profile, she often sighed (dramatically, to herself), but real, true, nonetheless. Perhaps part of the problem, which had been suggested more than once by friends, coworkers, ex-boyfriends, and know-it-all cousins in various states of intoxication, was self-esteem. As in: she didn't have much. Nor did she ever have any grand ambitions—no dreams of becoming a doctor or lawyer or certified computer technician, like you're supposed to—and the idea of *being* someone or *doing* something for a living never really occurred to her until she'd had kids. And by then it was too late. Now, at the unsettling age of thirty-four she was both too old and too young, a caged in-between, and she realized there were certain things she would never become, places she'd never go. Too much time had passed. The trajectory was set. She had kids. This was it. This was her life. Locked in. And her life, out of necessity, had been simplified, reduced.

In some ways, though, this made matters easier, this narrowing down to kids and work, kids and work. Nothing else except those two constants. But her schedule allowed for no deviations whatsoever. Financially it was touch and go, paycheck to paycheck, the smoke and mirrors of credit, post-dated checks, playing it dumb and saying she hadn't received a second payment notice let alone a first. Last month it became all too clear that she no longer could afford childcare every day. So on Tuesdays and Thursdays her friend Connie picked up Kyle and Sean Casey at school in the afternoon, and then brought both boys to the apartment, where they had two hours by themselves before Ramona arrived home. Kyle had just turned ten, certainly not old enough—and needless to say not mature enough—to care for his little brother, but Ramona figured, hoped, it was only temporary, a couple of months or so until she got ahead a little.

She told the evil Cole kid to go home ("You cussed! You cussed! I heard you cuss!"), Kyle to get another shirt for his brother. Sean Casey appeared all right, yet she figured she better not be one of those negligent parents you read about or see weeping on TV after the fact. How easy, how natural it is to judge and condemn from afar. But people never know the details, thought Ramona. They never know what's behind everything. Better to take him to the hospital just to be sure.

Then she was back on the dreaded 605. The evening traffic had subsided somewhat, now a steady, streaming pulse of cars. She drove slowly, cautiously, as if transporting hazardous material. And it seemed important that she should obey the speed limit and navigate the geriatric Corolla with great care. The other cars zoomed by, oblivious, like always. Sean Casey's face was still red and puffy from all the crying. But he was over it, even laughing now, making elaborate fart noises with his hands, a newly acquired talent he'd learned from Kyle, who pawed around in the backseat and felt compelled to read out loud (very loud) every billboard or sign or evidence of language they passed. See: even a simple drive was not a simple drive. They had an agenda to keep up with, after all.

Ramona did her best to pretend she was a mother worthy of Hallmark card couplets and not lose it. She stuck to the far right lane, checking her speedometer frequently. What the hell—burning a kid, your very own brother. Had it come to this? Would it only continue to get worse and worse the older they got? Outside the moon loomed low and heavy in the sky like a large clenched fist. It was late November in Southern California (they lived in Norwalk, she worked in Alhambra), and because of the recent rains, the air looked and smelled almost natural and not completely compromised and polluted, which was nice for a change. The inside of the car, however, reeked of bleach, as it had for weeks, ever since Kyle thought it would be funny to pour out half the bottle on the way home from the market. One of his raids on her authority and patience, part of a long, evolving history of advances and retreats. Kyle always the instigator, Sean Casey following along, the younger brother falling under the spell of the older brother, Ramona's influence over Sean Casey diminishing further with each passing day.

As she drove, scanning for the hospital exit, squinting into the eternal rush of headlights and brake lights, she told herself to ignore the boys as well as the sound erupting periodically from the engine—a symphonic rattling that had surfaced a few days before and was getting progressively louder and that she'd been hoping would just go away but hadn't and there was also the fact that the spare tire had been on for like the last month or so. Please don't break down now, she begged, not on the freeway with my kids in the car and no Triple-A and it's dark and I have a date next week with Victor Nance and we're on our way to the hospital because my one kid tried to burn my other one.

She just about tore off Kyle's head when he asked if she could turn on the radio.

"Nature of the injury?" asked the nurse in the emergency room. She was a big woman, blues singer big, with the booming voice to match. She stood behind a circular counter amid stacks and stacks of color-coded file folders, filling out the proper forms without glancing up at Ramona. She had just finished with a shirtless teenager—sixteen, maybe seventeen, lurching his way toward adulthood—who now sat down in the only empty chair, pressing a towel to his bleeding head with one hand, holding a copy of *Us Weekly* with the other. The waiting room was packed. People were listening like this was TV.

"Accident," Ramona admitted.

"You're going to have to be more specific than that, you want any kind of help."

Ramona paused. The nurse had power, authority. You could tell she knew how to manage and control and not be tragic, or pitied, or easily overwhelmed. And people were listening, every word.

"Household accident," Ramona added, hoping that would be enough.

But it wasn't. Her answer caused the nurse to stop writing and actually look at Ramona, her eyes about as sunken as eyes can get, up and then back down to the paperwork.

"I'm not doing this for my health you know. This here's a j-o-b. And now you got folks waiting behind you, big surprise."

Ramona glanced over her shoulder, and there was an old man and an old woman, the man hooked up to one of those portable oxygen tanks on wheels.

"Okay, look," she said, her stomach grinding toward a higher gear. There were medicines she could take but she never did.

"This is the situation," she conceded. "It's this: My son, he tried to set my other son, my younger son here, Sean Casey, on fire. There. That's why we're here. That's the story. I want to make sure that he's all right."

The nurse didn't even flinch, continued writing. It was, after all, an emergency room. They heard about this kind of stuff all the time. And worse. Much worse. The kind of everyday deviant behavior and violence and brain-scratching mayhem that doesn't even make the news, that begs the question: why do people do the things they do?

"Have a seat and we'll call you," the nurse said finally.

But there were no seats. Ramona took Sean Casey by the hand and walked him over to some available wall space near the bathrooms. The bleeding teenager nodded. Kyle was gone, disappeared. Probably off vandalizing million-dollar machinery or giving hotfoots to dying cancer patients. This was a boy with severe attachment and abandonment issues, who also had difficulty regulating his emotions. That's what the bearded school psychologist had said when he handed her a detailed fifteen-page report about her screwed-up son.

They waited for over three hours, got a seat after two. Phones rang and no one answered them. Another nurse replaced the one who had checked them in. The bleeding teenager plowed through four more magazines before someone at last called his name. The fluorescent lights hummed relentlessly. The man with the oxygen tank said, "I could die and nobody would even notice." Strange, terrible aromas drifted in and out of the area—bodies? blood? puss? fluids? dried skin, if that even had a smell? Every now and then a moan reverberated from somewhere down the hall, somewhere unseen. Since they hadn't eaten dinner, she gave the boys money for the vending machines. They gorged on Mars bars and Hawaiian Crisp potato chips. Sean Casey asked if they could have candy bars and chips for dinner every night. There was a word carved into the arm of her chair. The word was POOP.

She picked up an old issue of *National Geographic* and tried reading an article about the majestic lions of Africa who, turns out, sometimes eat their young. But she didn't get past the third paragraph. She couldn't read. She couldn't talk to the kids. She couldn't sleep. She couldn't do anything but just sit there. The walls were painted a glaring, oppressive white, not very conducive to contemplation. It was dead time, pure waiting. A sign said: *If you think you are PREGNANT tell the ER staff.*

After examining Sean Casey for less than a minute, the doctor (baby-faced, frat boyish, a slight stutter when he started in with the medical jargon) said her son was fine, there'd been no permanent injury, no trauma, no scarring, here's some ointment to be applied so-and-so times a day, etc., but she was right in coming in because you never know. Which was true—*you never do know*, that phrase sticking with her like a toothache—but the visit would probably cost like a couple grand because she was still under a probationary period at work and didn't have health benefits yet. The coverage wouldn't kick in until next month, that is if they decided to keep her on, and now that it looked as if she would have to spurn her boss's romantic advances, her future employment prospects with DataCorp appeared pretty bleak indeed. Then it would be back to temping and odd jobs and even more creative financial maneuvering until she could find something permanent. Any unexpected catastrophe could crush her and the boys. And plus that damn noise the car was making. Was it really getting louder or was that just her own paranoia? Taking it in might have to be put off. But what if something were to happen before that? She didn't want to die on a freeway, a single mother in heavy debt, with way too many credit cards and receding gums and an un-aerobicized ass. Lately she'd gotten into the habit of saying a little nondenominational prayer every time she slipped behind the wheel (it couldn't hurt), something like *please God just one more time just get me where I'm going this one last time and I'll promise to take the car in soon and to be a better person and be a better mother and do your will whatever that may be I'm open to suggestions and ashes to ashes and dust to dust and amen.*

The exit to the parking lot was next to the gift shop. People were buying flowers, liqueured truffles, balloons in the shape of a heart. Ramona stood in the long line (what time was it anyway?) and bought some gum for Sean Casey. He always had to have gum, or at least know that it was readily available, or the world lost its meaning. Ramona was annoyed with the boy's compulsion yet also sympathized with his raw need for such a balm, his desire for solace, no matter how meager, wherever he could find it. Once the glass exit doors had swished open, the boys bolted in the direction of the car and Sean Casey tripped twice (almost getting clipped by an SUV backing out of a parking space) and Kyle got there first and proceeded to jump on the Corolla's weathered hood to celebrate his victory.

She didn't know what she wanted to do but she certainly didn't want to go home, not back to the apartment and the faulty appliances, the water-stained ceilings, the old-lady wallpaper, the windows they'd never been able to open, the mysterious odor she'd never been able to get rid of (the gloomy reek of other lives, other renters, the people who lived there before you and had conversations and cooked meals and fucked and fought and made up in the same rooms where you're doing the exact same things, she'd decided after unsuccessfully employing countless air fresheners and probably Alzheimer's-causing sprays). There was that familiar slow burning inside her, that nameless smoldering signifying something just beyond her comprehension, the intensity of which varied depending on her mood, and her mood at the moment was not good, not good at all, but the question of what to do about it, the burning, remained just that, a question, and so she just wanted to drive—to drive somewhere. Anywhere. To be young and stupid and light again. No more of this constant heaviness. Had there ever been a time when that wasn't the case? Was thirty-four really that old? And then an idea began to insinuate itself, one that, truth be told, had crossed her mind on more than one occasion, usually after a couple of Long Island Iced Teas with her friend Larissa at the two-for-one happy hour at Shenanigan's. The idea being: gather the boys, drive somewhere far, far away, come to a stop, look around, open the door, listen to the wind, admire the consuming black of the sky, sit back, breathe, let go, let it come…Simple as that. Everything changes. Abandonment equals freedom.

When she got to the car Kyle was still stomping around on the hood like one of those Riverdance guys and Sean Casey was pouting and saying his knee hurt and maybe they should go back in the hospital and she knew there was nothing she could do about it, any of it, that this was the dynamic that was in place. Yet another sad commentary on her ever eroding parenting skills.

"I won," said Kyle.

"I'm starting the car in two seconds whether you're inside or not," Ramona said.

"So I guess we didn't need to come then." Kyle pushing it because he was Kyle. This was what he did. This was what made him Kyle.

"Two seconds," she snapped.

The boys had different fathers. So there were two fathers, two sons, and three sets of overbearing, told-you-so grandparents. And her. She was the center, the magnetic pull of this tiny, troubled universe.

In theory it worked like this: Kyle was with his father one weekend and she would have Sean Casey. The next weekend Sean Casey was with his father and she would have Kyle. Unless of course one of the fathers—she married the first but had the sense not to marry the second—couldn't be bothered on their particular weekend, which had been happening more often and which meant that her weekends were becoming just as chaotic and crisis-filled as her weeks. It was like she was underwater, forever submerged, coming up for gasping breaths of air that kept getting shorter, less substantial. She was too nervous and too distracted to go on dates. Her sister from time to time provided her with the names and numbers of good Christian men who lived in the area. At one particular low point Ramona actually called one of them. She left a message (Ted? Tad?), but he never called back. And next Thursday night she would be sharing a plate of fried zucchini sticks with Victor, pretending to be interested in the wisdom of the Jedi.

But now she was driving.

They hadn't encountered another car for a while. She was tired. Tired but exhilarated, pleasantly loopy. After escaping the tangle of several different freeways (the 605 to the 5 to the 710), they had been driving east on the 10 for more than an hour, the increasing space and distance allowing her to focus, to experience a new clarity in her thoughts, how one flowed so remarkably, so purposefully, to the next. The road hurled toward her, through her. It seemed as if something had finally been decided, had snapped Lego-like into place, a better fit, definitely, and that was a major relief. They were past Fontana now, past the new outlet stores, beyond the old refineries. That was about right— far enough but not too far—in Ramona's estimation. She slowed the car (the death rattle noise scratching louder as she did so) and parked on the shoulder. Both boys were in the back seat, unseatbelted, because what did it matter now. Sean Casey was asleep and Kyle hadn't said a word for the last forty minutes.

"Get out and pee," she told the rearview mirror.

"But I don't have to go," said Kyle.

"I don't care. Just take your brother and get out of the damn car and go try and pee."

"What if I can't?"

"Then you stand there and wait until you can."

She was practically screaming by now.

"Where are we going anyway? This is a gyp."

"Las Vegas. Now go piss."

The highway was empty, no other cars in sight. Steam rose from the hood of the embattled Corolla. There was a shooting pain in both of Ramona's hands that hadn't been there before. Whatever was happening was happening. This was her life. The headlights cut deep into the darkness, puncturing the night like a scalpel. She gripped the wheel and kept squeezing and tried to see as far ahead into the distance as she possibly could.

Kyle woke up his dumb-ass little brother and grabbed him by the hand and led him out into the desert. They were far from home, he didn't know where. It was cold and late and a school night to boot and he didn't have a jacket. His mother hadn't thought of that, just like she didn't think of everything until later, until it was over and done with and you were already on to the next thing. He heard the car door slam closed. Then the engine revved. His stomach felt funny. Like a broke washing machine that goes too fast and won't stop. Sean Casey trailed behind, his hand warm, soft, girlish. He continued walking, guiding his brother through the brush and dirt, but kept looking back over his shoulder. His mother sat slumped over the steering wheel, her back rising up and down like a wounded animal. The windows were getting fogged. Soon he wouldn't be able to see her.

He didn't know why he decided to burn his brother. It was just one of those things. It just happened and then it was over and then you could say that you'd done it. Cole had tried to burn his sister once but her clothes wouldn't catch fire. He went through a whole pack of matches before he gave up. When she told on him, Cole's mother pulled out her cigarette lighter and held it to his arm until it made a mark.

It would be hard to pee. He'd gone at the hospital. There was nothing left. And plus he had to deal with Sean Casey who didn't know anything, who still called it his wee-wee. Kyle heard something, something high-pitched and remote, maybe screaming, he thought at first, but probably just the wind. Sean Casey had snot running down over his mouth and onto his shirt, the baby. He was always leaking something—snot or tears or blood from picking a scab. Kyle stopped walking and looked back again and his mother hadn't moved, still humped over like that. He wondered if she was having trouble breathing, if he'd gone too far this time. It was so cold you could see your breath like maybe it smelled. He unzipped his pants and waited. His brother stood there like a retard, staring off into space and thinking whatever it is that retards think. "Pee, you reject," Kyle yelled, but Sean Casey didn't move. He started crying instead. The car was just sitting there, the sound of the engine becoming louder, briefly, before it got covered over by a bigger gust of wind, which made Kyle cross his arms for warmth, hugging himself. How long would he have to take care of his brother, and how long would he have to deal with his mother? Years. It would be years still. He hugged himself harder even though it wasn't doing much good.

Kyle turned away from the highway then, turned toward the desert, toward the open sky and the stars—the stars that seemed so close you could stick out your tongue and taste them, each one different, each one a wonderful new surprise. The future was out there, in front of him, somewhere, and one day it would come.

THE RIOT AND RAGE
THAT LOVE BRINGS

THE RIOT AND RAGE
THAT LOVE BRINGS

ON THE EPISODE OF *Cops* originally airing October 3, 2007, Delinda Slater can be seen answering a knock on her front door wearing shorts and a snug yellow tank top and holding a pair of scissors. She'd been cutting up John's underwear. This because of a fight they'd had earlier, one that turned out to be way worse than any of their previous Ali-Frazier bouts, the kind of epic blowout that gets talked about for years after. There'd been escalation all week; and she'd sensed something was coming, something ugly and final. The day had gone from bad to worse to truly fucked. Yelling, threats, taunts. Then some shoving, an errant punch or two. What was the fight about? She later couldn't even remember. It started over nothing, some shit little thing, and grew from there like a tornado that gets bigger and meaner. The heat and the weather didn't help either, just T.N.T. on top of everything else. Del's mother was out back with Savannah, Del's eight-year-old A.D.D. daughter. ("I don't believe in that A.D.D. crap," John once said. "They didn't have that when I was a kid.") To beat the heat, her mother turned on the hose and kept trying to coax the girl toward the spray to cool down, but Savannah didn't want any part of that, had never liked water, one of those particular kids who only eat certain foods and wear certain clothes. Del's mother warned, "I got the cordless out here, I'll call 9-1-1 if it doesn't stop." It didn't stop. "Call the cops, see if I care," said John, who'd never warmed to Tina and vice-versa. He'd been living there for almost a year, supposedly temporary.

Del freaked and shut the door on the cops. This was not good.

There were two of them, a lady cop and a man cop, and they got really pissed that she'd shut the door. After she let them back in she saw the camera and the guy holding it. The lady cop shouted, "Drop the weapon!" and Del kept wondering *what weapon, what weapon,* and then she realized the lady cop meant the scissors. So she dropped them. And that was when they, both the lady cop and the man cop, tackled her, cuffed her, facedown now, with hands pinned tightly behind her and struggling to breathe. The carpet smelled like Cheetos and cat. She glanced up and there was her mother crying and her daughter standing there (statue-like, mouth open) and she thought: so this is what it's all come down to, this is the train wreck that is my life, this is the riot and rage that love brings. Or if not love, then the attempt at love, which is all the more dangerous. When it's not the real thing. When it's an imposter.

The cops dragged her to her feet, started walking her outside. Del looked around as if she wouldn't be coming back. The house was a shitty one, there wasn't much to appreciate, but it was her house nonetheless, and all of a sudden she was overcome by a wave of longing. The TV was still going. On the floor she saw the scissors and the bits of John's BVDs, strewn about like sad little wishes you know will never come true. She usually dated men who wore boxers. His socks would have been next. After that she didn't know. She hadn't gotten that far.

Outside it was still hot—"hot as Satan's sauna," as one of her stepfathers used to say. The sun was going down, had finally given up, and the sky was a melting swirl of red and orange and purple. She loved the sky at this time of day, the bigness of it, especially during the summer, when there's something different about the light, when the colors seem to linger longer, to suggest something better might be coming even when you had no reason to think otherwise.

The lady cop steered her toward the cop car. She had her hair pulled back and she was pretty. Del wondered why she'd become a cop, being pretty and all, there was probably a story there, and she wanted to ask her this very question but the lady cop was the one asking the questions: what happened, where was John, why did you slam the door, did you know that resisting arrest is an arrestable offense? Meanwhile the man cop jogged down the street to look for John, who'd taken off on foot and didn't have his wallet or anything so he couldn't have gotten far; plus, he was barefoot. Maybe he was over at Frank Arroyo's, two houses down, drinking beer and watching satellite. Maybe he had walked over to the creek that no longer had any water. There weren't many places to go. It was a couple of miles into town and The Frog Pond and its classic rock jukebox.

Neighbors had gathered on the sidewalk. Whenever Del breathed, her chest ached. She told herself to be calm.

Was arrestable a word? Del wondered.

The lady cop asked more questions: her name, had she been drinking today, had she taken any drugs, what had happened here, who was at fault. And the guy with the camera. He was there, too. Filming everything.

"Now, is this your husband we're talking about?" the lady cop said.

"No."

"Boyfriend, then?"

Del looked at the camera guy. But she couldn't see his face. Just the camera. And the bright light attached to it.

"Yeah, I guess," said Del. "Boyfriend, sure. Though it's not like anything official."

"What do you mean?"

"Just...there's issues. It ain't all roses and champagne."

"Nothing ever is," said the lady cop, and Del agreed, and for a brief moment they were in the same place in their heads, two women agreeing and nodding about the disappointments of men.

"Did he hit you?" the lady cop then asked.

Del thought about lying and saying it was all John. It wouldn't be the first time she lied to a cop. And why not fuck John up? But she couldn't lie. Not this time, for whatever reason.

"It was mutual."

"Ma'am, let me tell you something and I want you to listen. Are you listening?"

Del nodded.

"We get a call for a domestic and we don't know what we're gonna find. You go into people's lives, you go into their houses, and you never know what's going on behind them doors. Can you understand that?"

"Yes," Del said.

"Look, I don't know you from boo. You could be Mrs. Hannibal Lecter for all I know. You could have a gun, you could have a knife. I need to protect myself and I need to protect you. I'm going to arrest you, Ma'am. You are going to go to jail tonight."

Del was crying now. She didn't want her daughter to see her like this. That seemed like the most important thing right now. Jail was fine. Jail was acceptable. Just keep Savannah inside the house. Protect her daughter. If she could do one good deed in her life, something that would be her ticket to heaven and redemption, it would be that: protect her daughter. From this. From everything. From the world and all that she couldn't control, which was plenty.

Later they arrested John down at The Frog Pond. His shirt was off. He went down fighting, yelling, "I'm not going to jail, I'm not going to jail for nothing or nobody. I'm innocent. Motherfuckers. You can't prove a thing."

That got filmed, too.

Everyone had to sign a release form saying it was okay to show them on TV when the episode aired. If they didn't sign, their faces would be blurred out. Del's mother didn't sign, so she got blurred. And Savannah, too, because she was a kid. John and Del signed. Sent all the paperwork to the *Cops* producer person in L.A. and told their friends and waited.

The phone was ringing. Del almost let the machine get it, but then she thought it might be her friend Charlene who owed her money. John was one of those guys who was good at ignoring the phone. She picked up.

"It's on, it's on! You guys are on! Shit! They just showed the preview part and it's the one with you guys. John, he's really put on some pounds. He should really wear a shirt, Del."

It wasn't her friend Charlene; it was her friend Stephanie who did not owe her money. Three months had passed since the night Del cut up John's underwear, the night Del thought was a turning point. The episode of *Cops* was on at last, tonight, while her mom and Savannah were out running errands and getting ice cream. John sat sprawled like a teenager on the couch watching something boring about the anniversary of an old baseball game. It was a big deal apparently (to those who cared). Del in and out of the living room, watching, not watching, seeing the game and the crowd and the players in black and white and thinking how different her life would be if she'd been living back then, before *Cops* and computers and cell phones and everything else that made life more complicated, more sad somehow. But maybe it wouldn't have been any different, except for the clothes and haircuts. Men like John had been around since the dawn of time.

"Turn it to Fox," she told him. "Stephanie says it's on, finally. I'll get the VCR going."

John switched it over to Channel 6 while Del popped in a blank tape. There was that commercial for the exercise contraption that, after just six weeks, created a brand-new you. Del couldn't help but crack a smile. That was her—the brand-new Del—after she got home from jail, two days in there before her mother could scrape the money together, and she swore—fucking swore—that the soap opera of Del and John had ended. And now he was still here. It got better after, then a little worse, then back to a little better. He was working now, which helped. They went to Vegas; Savannah chipped a tooth; Del's sister miscarried; and they eventually agreed to drop the charges against each other, call it good.

"It's kind of trippy," John said.

"Kinda," she agreed, sitting down in one of the chairs instead of next to him on the couch.

"Wait—shit. We need beers for this." John ran to the kitchen. And while he was gone, Del considered the indentation on the couch where his body had been, his trace, his invisible weight.

She thought about how for such a long time she liked to believe that she kept her heart locked inside a box, and that there was a key that could open this box, and that also she had to be careful about who could and could not have this key, or keys; the different guys coming and going who had been able to find a key, click something open inside of her *like so*. Every time always the last time. She was not that careful apparently, John being the latest example. He had the key and sometimes she didn't know why. She wasn't the smartest person in the world. But she wasn't the stupidest either.

John returned and replanted himself on the couch, handed her one of the Coors Lights.

"You wanna call anybody?" he asked. He was staring straight ahead, stubble on his chin and jaw, his face red and blurry from the sun.

How many times could you be wrong about love?

"Naw, let's not," Del said. "I thought I would. But now it doesn't seem right. Let's just watch it."

Then the *Cops* song came on (*Bad boys, bad boys, whatcha gonna do?*) and she waited to see herself, to see what her life would look like there on the screen.

A MATTER OF
TWENTY-FOUR HOURS

A MATTER OF TWENTY-FOUR HOURS

PORTER'S MOTHER HAD BEEN dying for years, a seemingly never-ending downward spiral, but now it was really happening. After this last relapse, the doctors said there wasn't anything more they could do. They said to look into hospice. They said if she left the hospital it would be a matter of twenty-four hours, maybe forty-eight if they were lucky.

This information was not firsthand; it was secondhand, from his brother, Emmett, who was at the hospital dealing with the paperwork to get their mother home and finding a hospice nurse who could be available as soon as possible. Porter was at the bar, his usual Thursday night shift, presiding over another evening of anonymous drinking and forgetting. There were only half a dozen or so customers. Every TV tuned to a different station. When he saw his brother's number appear on his cell phone, he almost didn't answer it.

"So this is it, Porter. You understand that? This is it. She's coming home to die. She wants to die at home. She wants to see her plants and flowers one more time. She'd like to see her youngest son, too, if it isn't too much of an inconvenience for you."

Porter concentrated on a customer he'd had his eye on for a while, the lone woman. She swayed in front of the jukebox after having made a selection—the Stones, a fairly obscure track from *Exile on Main Street*, "Shine a Light," something only a die-hard would pick, which made her all the more alluring. She swayed and danced like she had a different body, one that was younger and thinner, that fit into jeans better, that got her the things she wanted or thought she wanted, but she was okay with all that, the music filled her with whatever she lacked.

"I'll try," he told his brother. "I'll see what I can do."

"She'll be dead tomorrow, Port. I don't know how I can make it any clearer than that."

And just then a man entered the bar and came up to the Stones woman and gave her a deep, drunken kiss. That was that. Once again, someone else had made the decision for him.

One hand—he could count the girlfriends he'd ever had, including high school, on one hand. Some (index finger, ring finger) not really even girlfriends. Just girls he'd somehow known and also somehow, usually through circumstance, or alcohol, or both, managed to sleep with. Once. Or twice. Or once. One hand.

"You don't even know yourself, who you really are, who you are as, like, a person," one girl told him without any prompting whatsoever.

"What do you care about?" asked another one. "I mean really care. What are you passionate about?"

He thought for a while, considering not answering but then did.

"Drinking," he said. "I care about drinking. I'm passionate about that."

He meant it to be funny, but as soon as the words left his mouth he knew it wasn't.

"That's sad," said the girl, whose name was Claudia and who wasn't a girl at all but a thirty-eight-year-old woman with two shit kids, an auto-immune disorder, and teeth gone yellow from smoking too much.

He couldn't help himself, though. He felt like he had something to give, if only he could find the right person. The right person would make all the difference. The right person would save him. And much time and effort and energy had been wasted over the years because of this belief.

As with the others, he and Claudia didn't keep in touch after.

The clock at the bar ran twenty minutes fast, time eternally accelerated so that people would vacate earlier than two a.m. It wasn't closing time yet, but the place had emptied out, and Porter wanted to move things along. He had to decide: was he going to his mother's or not? He had to decide and fairly soon. There was a bit of a deadline here. His brother had called two hours ago. The clock was ticking. His mother was dying, actually dying this time. All the previous false alarms. He never thought it would happen. He had to decide.

Porter toweled down the bar one more time. He'd spent so much time at The Alibi as a customer, as a dedicated drinker, that the owner, Marco, finally asked him if he wanted a job. Besides bartending, Porter also did construction for a friend's company, but the last job had been months ago and his friend kept saying there would be more work soon, soon, things were bound to pick up, just hang in there, the fucking economy, what can you do? Another friend used to get him drywall work but that had dried up, too.

"Drink up, folks," Porter called out. "Bar's closing in ten. Closing in ten."

The only customers left did not stir, two older men in a booth, drinking Rolling Rock and staring vacantly and not really talking to each other, more like enduring the other's presence. A group of dreadlocked hippie kids (he'd carded them, taken their crumpled dollar bills and greasy change) had left when Johnny Cash came on the jukebox. You never knew if these kids were students at Humboldt State or just hanging out, living the life, mistakenly thinking it was still the Summer of Love.

Deadline. The word made sense now. That's probably how the word originated. Someone was going to die. Something was at stake. There was a before and after, and after the after, after the line was or wasn't crossed, there would be consequences—consequences that would be felt for a very long time. There was impact. You couldn't ignore what came after the deadline had passed.

He went to the bathroom to clean up. When he opened the stall door, he found a regular in there, Frank, passed out on the toilet, his pants and underwear bunched sadly around his ankles, head jabbed back, snoring up a shit storm. Frank could have been fifty-five, could have been eighty. It was hard to tell.

"Frank, come on. Wake up."

Porter gave him a nudge in the shoulder. That did the trick.

"What? Oh. Wait. Oh shit. What happened, Tex?"

"You fell asleep on the crapper."

"Oh. Oh no. Wait. Shit. What was it? What was it I was just saying? I was just telling someone something, maybe it was you even, I was just telling them that my daughter, the other day she shows up and she's bought me a computer. A computer. She says it'll give me something to do, I need that in my life, it'll give me something to do and I can get the Internet and I can look up all sorts of things, things I've always been curious about but never had the time and now I have the time. She opens the box and starts setting it up. Computers. They're about as useless as tits on a bull. I ask her, I ask her for the gift receipt. I ask her when she gives me the computer. Oh, she doesn't like that at all. My daughter. She gets pissed. She gets all pissy. Like she does. She could lose a few pounds and maybe things would be better for her. I don't know. I worry about her. But that's what a parent does. Was you the one I was telling all this to?"

"Wasn't me, Frank."

"Thought it was you. Must have been some other young guy."

"Young? Me? I don't feel young."

"Shit. Don't talk to me. You're young. When you're looking at what I'm looking at, then come back and talk to me. Then you'll know what's old."

"You drive tonight, Frank?"

"I didn't walk, that's for sure."

"Come on. I'll give you a ride. Closing soon. Pull up your goddamn pants."

"What? You my mommy now?"

"Let's go. You can get your car tomorrow."

"Hell. All right. Would suck to die in a car crash at this point."

"That would suck."

"You okay with a girl with a little meat on her bones, Tex? My daughter's name is Pamela. She's a good person. A better person than me. That's something, at least. One generation better than the next. She ever give me a grandchild then we'll really be talking. You interested?"

"I'm good, Frank. Thanks anyway."

"Change your mind you let me know. She's been to France. She doesn't wear no jewelry though."

"I'll keep it in mind."

"You do that. You let me know. She's a good woman. Hey. I think I've got a bit of a gravity situation here. I could sure use some help with these pants, Tex."

Before he left the bar, he got a text from his brother: *Come. Now. Last chance. Hospice nurse here soon. Don't be a dick all your life.*

Frank's place was down in Eureka, so Porter drove that lonesome stretch of 101 between Arcata and Eureka, Humboldt Bay off to the right, the water black and looming, Frank dozing like the drunk that he was, drizzle coming down in one long steady sigh, reminding Porter that he had to replace his windshield wiper blades. The apartment just as sad as he'd imagined. That old man smell. That old man desperation and finality. Nominal furniture. Food-crusted dishes. Dim lights. Clothes everywhere, a vast spawn of ancient underwear and socks. Prescriptions, medicines, creams, ointments. Empty booze bottles. Newspapers probably dating back to Clinton. Stacks of unopened mail on a TV tray, the only thing resembling a table in the entire apartment. A fishbowl without fish, filled instead with paper receipts and change, mostly pennies, it seemed. Frank murmuring something about his disability checks not coming on time anymore. The goddamn government. The goddamn people at the bar who were out to get him. It sounded like the neighbors upstairs were having a party. Old people creeped Porter out, always had. Music pumping. *Boom-boom. Boom-boom.* Like a heartbeat. It didn't stop.

He deposited Frank onto his bed, which was only a mattress on the floor of a shoebox-sized bedroom, and the floor itself was covered with more of his old man sheddings: clothes, boxes, papers, the computer Frank had told him about earlier. Porter didn't bother with taking off Frank's clothes, just made sure he fell asleep on his stomach, then placed a glass of water next to the mattress, and left. The decision still hadn't been made. For now, he was just driving. Aimless, teenage driving. He followed the gravitational suck of his headlights for a while. All through Eureka and then back on 101, the drizzle sometimes stopping but always returning. He pulled over at a gas station. That was at least a decision he could make. He needed gas. And he was hungry. Close to three a.m. now. The cold early morning air stunned him, like an electric shock, as he stepped out of his car.

Porter rushed inside, grabbed a frozen burrito, microwaved it for too long, thing was burning hot, paid for it, and also put five dollars on pump six, scorching his tongue as he ate the burrito and pumped his gas. Back inside the car, he didn't start the engine. He sat there and stared at the glowing mini mart. The lights inside. All the food and booze and motor oil. It was too late for many customers to be there, but he kept waiting for someone to walk in, for something to happen. The door: it would open. Someone would walk in and the world would start again. It was that simple. All someone had to do was open the door and walk through it, cross that threshold. He kept waiting. It was good to know that such a place existed, that if you needed any of the basics at any time during the day or night, you could get them, twenty-four hours a day, always available, as long as you could pay. All you had to do was walk through the door.

His mother's house was up in McKinleyville, which meant he'd have to drive farther north, pass the bay again, this time on his left, through Arcata and beyond the airport (where planes frequently hit deer on the runway), plus a main street, plus side streets, then a sleepy cul-de-sac, twenty minutes, tops, if he left right now.

Fact: He'd always been the fuck-up brother, the one who deviated and exasperated and could not be tamed—that role had felt natural, he knew the lines, how to be. In high school, Emmett played football and saved money to buy a car, while Porter smoked dope and taught himself bass guitar. It was a study in contrasts, hard to believe they'd come from the same parents, although there wasn't much evidence about their father, a mystery man who'd disappeared when they were very young and occasionally sent checks and age-inappropriate birthday gifts, Emmett more like his mother, a good citizen, a reliable soul, and so Porter assumed he got what he got from his father, whose last known address was Tampa, Florida.

When his mother started getting sick, Emmett had been the one who took care of everything. The doctor appointments and the specialists and the health insurance. His brother had a wife, kids, an office job, a regular life with many responsibilities, and still he stepped in and found the time, made it work. Porter, on the other hand, flinched, receded farther from his family. He wasn't there yet as a person. Not capable of that kind of sacrifice. He drank more, spoke less. Listened to the vast echo his life had become. Whenever Emmett cornered him on the subject of his unavailability, all Porter could manage to say was: "I can't do it. I'm sorry. I can't."

The first stroke happened on her birthday, at a restaurant, the Sweet River Grill and Bar in the Eureka Mall. Both Porter and Emmett were there, along with Emmett's family, a fairly silent celebration of her sixty-fourth year. One moment she was ordering chicken fajitas and the next she was unable to speak. She kept opening her mouth, fish-like, but nothing came out. They drove her to the hospital and waited and Emmett's wife took the kids home and they waited some more and then the emergency room doctor informed them that she'd had a stroke. He also told them that there was this drug called TPA, which is a real miracle drug, which can help prevent any after affects the stroke might cause. But it could also kill her. It was a fifty-fifty chance. So they had to make a decision right then and there: give her the drug (and potentially, maybe, help her after, but also maybe kill her) or not give her the drug (and she likely wouldn't be able to speak normally after, would also possibly experience partial or full paralysis on the right side of her body). Porter and Emmett just standing there. The doctor waiting. The nurse, the assistants. Everyone waiting. It almost made Porter laugh. How could they make such a decision? His mother's life literally in their hands.

"Can we have a few minutes to talk?" Emmett asked.

"Yes, but that's about all you have," said the doctor, who was wearing a leather jacket. "Every minute here counts. The longer we wait to give her the drug, the more likely the effects of the stroke will be more significant."

The doctor and his jacket and the others left.

"Porter, what do you think?"

He couldn't say anything. He stared at his mother's open mouth. He might have muttered, "I don't know." He might have not. Machines hummed and beeped. They were surrounded by a white curtain, no walls or doors, all sounds entering. In the bed next to them, a man moaned, said he couldn't feel anything in his legs, *they were dead, dead legs*, he said, and a woman said *they're still here, see?* TPA stood for something but it hadn't sunk in. His mother didn't move. His mother who had raised two sons, who hadn't dated after their father left, who had given up on men, who had worked two jobs for many years, sometimes three jobs during the holidays, and often, growing up, it was just the two of them, the brothers, the house all to themselves, an empty, lonely, guilty place.

The doctor came back. It seemed odd: an emergency room doctor wearing a leather jacket. Porter wanted to ask him about it but didn't.

"Have you decided?" the doctor said.

Emmett looked at Porter one more time. Nothing.

"Give her the drug," Emmett said, and they did, and she lived.

After that, he retreated further from his family, vanishing for long stretches—minimal contact, infrequent phone calls, even more infrequent visits. His mother pulled through the stroke, physical therapy for six weeks and then she was pretty much back to where she was before. He was living in Fortuna at that point, until a friend lured him up to Bandon, Oregon, where he picked cranberries and drank vodka gimlets and tried to love a waitress.

He wasn't sure how long he'd be gone. The friend also had a

friend who picked morel mushrooms and was apparently making a small fortune. The friend of a friend was part of a group that roamed Oregon's forests in the spring, after the snow thawed, looking for these highly prized, highly priced fungi. The friend said he could get them into the group and they'd be set. Promises were made. The morel people were a tight-knit group, heavy into hash and Cat Stevens. To pick the mushrooms in Oregon, you had to have a permit, but the morel people did not have any permits. Porter and his friend met them—about ten in all—at a camp site in the Cascades for a weekend trip. A hippie woman named Heaven asked him if his energy was balanced. He said he didn't think so. Another person told him how you had to respect the morels, acknowledge their feelings and history.

The group, Porter learned, tracked forest fires because the mushrooms thrived in areas that had been burned out; fir and pine forests were the best. They had maps and timelines and botany books—for hippies, they were surprisingly well organized. There was, as expected, a fair amount of hash, plus several ponytail guys, one of whom strummed a guitar and sang "Peace Train" and "Moonshadow." Later he discovered that the weekend was some kind of test, to see if they fit in or something. His friend had passed. He did not. It was never clear why.

And no matter how many times he washed his hands he could never completely remove the stain from the cranberries, always a faint pinkish-red clinging to his fingertips. The ships in Bandon's small harbor swayed in the ocean's unknown currents; few of the neglected vessels ever went anywhere, it seemed. Eventually he returned to Humboldt, feeling like it might be getting out of hand now, the years of vague, inconsequential drift, time passing by and somehow accumulating.

There was another stroke, additional diagnoses, recurrent treatments, and physical and mental decline. Just coordinating the pill and medication schedule alone was staggering, his brother complained whenever he had a chance, which wasn't very often.

The last time Porter spoke to his mother, she told him how she couldn't pee straight anymore, her stream unpredictable and going every which way, the humiliation of this, yet another failure of the body.

•

A woman answered the door.

"Hi," said Porter.

"Hello," the woman replied, an accent he couldn't place, her hair pulled back and piled high atop her head and held in place by a series of pins and a brightly colored headband. Had his mother already died? Was he too late? Had someone else already moved in?

"I'm Porter," he said, explaining, immediately wondering why he had to explain anything to a stranger—but if not to a stranger, he thought, then who else?

"Oh yes, yes, Por-ter," the woman repeated slowly. "The other son. The other brother, Emm-ett, he told me about you. Yes, yes. You come in now, please."

Once he was inside the small entryway, there stood his brother. Waiting. Eyes red-rimmed. Heavy stubble. Looking simultaneously pissed and relieved at seeing Porter. The same perpetual scowl he'd had as a boy and had never lost. There was no formal greeting.

The woman who'd answered the door took Porter's jacket and disappeared down the hallway, the house dark and quiet. It was around four a.m. now. Only a few lights were on, and the rain's volume increased, more water coming down now that he was inside. He smelled coffee. When Porter had arrived for work at The Alibi—that seemed like another day, another lifetime ago. Somewhere, he had an apartment. Somewhere, there was junk mail waiting to be opened. Somewhere, there was a life for him. He would try to get there. And by doing this, by being here now, he had a better chance. And that was something.

"She's who hospice sent," said Emmett. "She came right over. Margarita. She sings and hums. Ma likes it. She thinks she's an old cousin. Didn't know we had any Indonesian blood in the family."

"That's where she's from?"

"Something like that. She's a little hard to follow, but like I said, she's helping Ma relax. And she's got beads. Those religious beads."

"Rosary beads? Did Ma get religious?"

"No, I don't think so."

"I bet that happens a lot, toward the end."

"Well, this is the end. Come on. Come say hi."

The hallway was a gauntlet. Like watching his life quickly pass before his eyes. Both walls decorated with framed photos of him and his brother, starting from when they were babies. Pictures of Emmett playing Little League, Emmett receiving an academic award; also pictures of him, Porter, perched unhappily atop an equally unhappy pony, another one as an angry teenager, defiantly gazing away from the camera, not wanting to be captured, staring off at some distant forgotten thing. In one of the pictures Emmett had braces. By the time it was Porter's turn, there wasn't enough money, and so he went through life with crooked teeth. Every time his tongue noted the resultant tilts and gaps, he thought of his brother.

The door to his mother's bedroom was open. She had one of those hospital beds that went up and down and had rails. They must have installed it at some point. Porter wanted to ask Emmett about this but caught himself, because there was his mother, ancient and ruined, body stretched out like a corpse. Her eyes were closed, her mouth open, and it seemed like this was how she was going to stay, it was over, she was done, he was too late, but when he reached out and touched her hand, her eyes flashed open, life still there, and she blinked and said, "Porter, Porter. You came."

Retractable. That was the word for the bed. When things go up and down, back and forth, one way and then the other.

"Hi, Ma."

His energy wasn't balanced. His energy was all over the place, fucked up and every which way, dispersed in ways he didn't understand.

"It's so good to see you, dear. And just in time. We have to get packed. We have to get ready."

"Oh yeah? Where you going, Ma?"

"Montana. Or Wyoming, maybe. There's something about those states. The wide openness, I guess. The space. I've been dreaming of that. I've always wanted to go there, to see that. Your father had a cousin there. In Montana. We always talked about visiting but never did. They have that geyser. Old Faithful. I'd like to see Old Faithful. Just stand there and watch and be amazed one last time."

Emmett leaned over, whispered: "Margarita said this is pretty common. Talking about a trip towards the end. It's normal. Just go with it."

Porter turned back to his mother. She still held his hand. Her voice was slow and drugged. And the more she talked, the slower she went, and the more pained she seemed.

"Montana," he said. "Sounds great."

"Porter, I've missed you. It's so good to see your face. You live so close by. And we never see each other. Or hardly. But now you're here. You're here."

"I'm here, Ma. I'm here now."

Then Margarita entered the room. She was in her mid-fifties mostly likely, efficient-bodied, a compact woman, bird-like in her movements, certain of her place in the world and what she needed to be doing. And what she needed to be doing was this: caring for a dying woman.

"Time for your medicine, Mrs. Schill-er. Open wide now. In it goes. Drop drop."

His mother obeyed, and Margarita produced a dropper from her pocket and administered two quick drops of a clear liquid into his mother's mouth.

"Five milliliters," Margarita instructed the brothers. "Every two hour. You watch. You do it next time. Por-ter or Emm-ett. Okay?"

"Morphine," Emmett told Porter. "It's the only thing that helps."

Margarita left and Porter looked at the sliding glass door that led to a small patio area where his mother kept her beloved plants and flowers. But it was dark out there. You couldn't see anything.

"Isn't there a light out on the patio?" asked Porter.

"It's not working."

"Is it the bulb?"

"No, it's not the bulb. I already tried that. It's the goddamn wiring or something. It's not working."

There was a moan: slow, deep, rising. It consumed the room. And it was not a sound that emanated from the woman who lay there now and who had given birth to them and sometimes—not often, but sometimes—let them fall asleep on the couch on Saturday nights while watching old movies; no, it came from someone, somewhere else. And it kept going, the moan. They paused until it passed. Then they paused some more. It was hard not to marvel at the otherworldly quality of the moan. Porter had never heard anything like it before.

"I thought you said she wanted to see her plants," said Porter.

"She does, Porter. It's all she's been talking about. Until you got here. Here she is dying and all she cares about is her goddamned plants. But I got enough going on with the morphine and Margarita and the Neptune Society. Besides, it'll be light soon. Not all that much longer."

"Wait. I've got an idea."

Porter walked to the kitchen, rummaged around in several drawers until he located what he was looking for: flashlights. There were three total. He took them and some masking tape, too. Back in the bedroom, he opened the sliding glass door and got to work. He taped two of the flashlights to the arms of a patio chair, set the third one on the seat. Then he angled the chair toward the plants and turned them all on. It worked. The patio was lit up enough to see what was out there.

"Is she awake?" he asked his brother when he was back inside.

"She's in and out. It's kind of hard to tell."

"Ma, you awake or asleep?"

"Awake," she said, opening her eyes.

"You can see your plants now."

They helped her sit up a bit more so she could see.

"Is that better, Ma?"

"Yes. Thank you."

He wondered: Could one positive act erase everything that had come before? Did it really work that way? No. Probably not. But it was a start. And sometimes it was just the right thing to do. Simple as that. Not symbolic. Not a sign. Not anything except what it was: kindness.

"And not just for the patio," his mother said. "But for coming."

"I'm sorry. I should've come sooner."

"You're here now."

She meant this. The words were true. They were a comfort.

"Just rest, Ma. Just enjoy your plants. You can see them now. You don't have to do anything else."

"There's some new bulbs. My tulips. I hadn't noticed."

Then she drifted off again, eyes closing, body seeping further into the bed.

"Why don't you get something to eat, Emmett. Take a shower. Whatever. Take a break. I'll sit with her."

"You sure?"

"I'm sure."

Porter settled into the chair by his mother's bed. The room was the same as it had been for years: simple, orderly, hardly a trace of the person who slept there. The walls mostly bare, the furniture brown and grandma-ish, a lone turquoise jewelry box that held little jewelry. There wasn't much for Porter to do except stare at the plants on the patio. Sleep would come at some point, but not yet. He thought of the woman at The Alibi, dancing to the Stones song, and then he thought of someone else. All that bursting greenery out there because of his mother's meticulous care, because of all the rain, all the cloud-filled days and nights here in Humboldt, this forgotten top half of California, this gloom-hearted weather that allowed everything to thrive.

The shower was now going in the hallway bathroom. His brother. Dishes stacking, cutlery clanking—that would be Margarita—in the kitchen. It was a tiny house. It had always been a tiny house. No sound a secret, no grudge ever completely hidden.

He sat and watched his mother sleep and thought of how he didn't know the names of any of the plants and flowers on the patio—maybe some ferns or something, but that was about it—and he also thought of how this small, shitty little thing, this minor lapse, not knowing the names, was as substantial as any of the larger failures in his life. The shitty little things added up. They meant something individually but also when taken in full. The next time his mother woke he would ask her to tell him the names, to recite them multiple times. They would say the names together. Repeat them like a chant or prayer. He would make the effort to remember and retain, and this, then, would be carried on, the names, passed down, from her to him, from mother to son, the names he would remember for all the years ahead, all the open, unknown time during which he would make up for everything in the past. He'd been awake almost twenty-four hours straight now.

Then he dozed for a while, he couldn't be sure how long, and when he awoke it was starting to get light, the day taking hold, and his mother was awake, too.

"I need more medicine," she said.

"I'll get Margarita."

"I want you to do it."

He went and got the morphine. Emmett was snoring away on the couch in the living room, Margarita at the kitchen table, reading her Bible.

"Two quick drops," she reminded him. "Drop drop. And tell her to swallow. Sometimes they forget. Swallow is very important."

By the time he got back to the room his mother's eyes were closed again. She was asleep.

"Ma? I've got the medicine."

She opened her mouth without opening her eyes, and Porter carefully administered the drug. Drop drop. Just like Margarita said. He watched his mother swallow, sigh. Then she wanted water, so he picked up the glass on her nightstand and put the plastic straw to her lips—lips so wasted and dry that he thought she'd take a long, thirst-quenching gulp, but all she could manage was a quick, one-second sip and she was done.

"Is that better?" he asked.

"Yes. Thank you. There's still pain but it's less pain with the medicine. Thank you."

Porter returned to the chair, not sure of what to do or say next.

"Do you want to talk?"

"No, not now," she said. "It hurts to talk. Everything hurts."

Outside on the patio: more growing gray light, birds fluttering and chirping, a view of the overgrown lawn and the back fence and the neighbor's roof and chimney. His mother had lived here for decades and soon she would not be here. Someone else would be in this same spot, looking out this sliding glass door, seeing the same things. This was fact. This was inevitable. But still, it didn't seem possible.

"But you can talk. Just keep talking. That would be nice. I'll listen."

"Just keep talking?"

"Yes."

"Like what? Anything?"

"Yes. Anything. I just want to hear your voice."

So Porter leaned back in the chair and thought of what he could say and then started talking, hoping that it would be enough.

STALLING

STALLING

MY SON, SIX, IS practicing dying. It's something he's started doing at bedtime, part of the nightly wind-down routine, when I read him books and he stalls because he doesn't want to go to sleep yet. So he pretends he's dying.

Lately I've been telling him about my father, who died two months before he was born. And along with telling him about my father, his grandfather, there have been the usual tricky questions about death: What happens to our bodies when we die? Where do we go? Do we know we're dead? Is it just like sleeping?

"Watch," he instructs me, gently lying himself down in his bed and flattening his arms against his sides, like a body in a coffin. "No, wait—now. Watch me now. See if you can see me breathing."

He holds his breath for as long as he can, about fifteen seconds, though it seems longer, his chest remaining flat and still, and he looks dead, enough so that it makes me hold my breath. Then his breathing returns in one big exhale and he coughs and it's over and he's asking more questions, stalling:

"What was I like when I was a baby?"

"What were you like when you were a baby, Daddy?"

"What was Mommy like when she was a baby?"

"What was Grandpa Ron like?"

I answer the questions. The last one is hard, though, even after all these years. I tell my son that his grandfather loved him very much, that he liked tennis, that he was funny and liked to joke, and that we're all very sad he's not here.

"We're sad?" my son asks.

"Yeah, we're sad," I tell him. "But it's okay to be sad. We just miss him."

He rolls over on his side, like he might finally be ready to sleep.

"I miss him, too," he says.

He breathes and closes his eyes. I hold my breath again. He doesn't move.

ROUGH

ROUGH

Anna told Aaron that she liked it kind of rough. They were walking back to his apartment, mildly drunk, shuddering against the streaming San Francisco fog and cold. He wasn't sure what that meant exactly, "kind of rough," but he didn't want to disrupt the flow of the potentially epic evening (so far so good) with stupid questions that would reveal his staggeringly sedate suburban roots and quasi-conservative leanings, which he still felt vaguely embarrassed about even after having lived in the famously liberal city—The City—for close to seven years now. That's what they called it here, The City, capital "T," capital "C," as in "I've been living in The City for close to seven years now," as if there was only one city and where else would you live?

As it turned out, though, whether or not Aaron was sexually qualified in the rough department didn't really matter. After a poorly executed elevator kiss (his initial overture got ear and hair instead of lips), and after opening a bottle of Kahlúa (the only alcoholic beverage he could forage in the kitchen—it was either that or NyQuil) and engaging in some subsequent sofa groping and minimalist dialogue right before (Should I?...There...How's that?...Maybe if...Okay, good...Wait...), he came in like five seconds and then it was over.

"So much for rough," he said, going for levity, because at that point what else could he do? And then because she didn't say anything back right away he added, "It's been a while."

"Me too," she said.

•

Aaron's brother gave the toast at the wedding. He was in A.A. so he didn't raise a glass of champagne. He raised a glass of water instead. The speech incorporated all the standard themes and conventions of the limited genre—the use of humor and embarrassment mixed, ultimately, when it came time for the 150 or so guests to uniformly hoist their glasses upward and wish the happy couple the best, with sincerity; covering Aaron's nontraumatic childhood, his bumbling yet endearing adolescence and teenage years, his partying college days (and here Aaron's brother inserted a cautionary note about the perils of excessive drinking, offering himself as an example), and his eventual relocation to The City, except Aaron's brother, being a lifelong Midwesterner, made the faux pas of saying the actual name; and then bringing in Anna, what a great girl she was, and how she made such a great addition to the whole curmudgeonly Cahill clan, and of course ending with the final thought of how now there was one family instead of two, etc.

Everyone agreed that the wedding was a major success (although, granted, the D.J. ignored Aaron and Anna's emphatic request *not* to play "Y.M.C.A."). Guests mingled easily, naturally; trays carrying wine and hors d'oeuvres kept appearing just when more food and drink were needed, as if on cue; time slowed to a tranquil, celebratory hum; and the outside world temporarily receded away like a spent wave returning to the ocean. And there was one point during the reception when Anna looked across the room and there was Aaron talking to a pregnant cousin of his and then he turned and their eyes met at just the right time and it was one of those totally clichéd yet very real cinematic moments (complete with orchestral soundtrack building in the background, or so it seemed to their mutual internal stereo system) where everything falls into place and you know you're doing the right thing and that people are meant for each other and no, we're not all essentially alone, and yes, a life can in fact be shared, truly, wholly, deeply.

Why do we say what we say, do what we do? Can reason and motive and certainty ever be completely confirmed? How does love begin? How does it end? Does it end at all? What, if anything, lasts? This was the babbling brook of thoughts and questions that flowed through her on the cab ride home, still dark, The City still asleep, but the night just about ready to expire, to become something else, the sky slowly lightening.

She didn't know why she said she liked it rough, which wasn't true, which was just a dumbshit line that came to her, an utterance penned by someone else and that slipped out by mistake. It was something to say when you're tipsy from too many cosmopolitans and your body is alive with the electric blood-buzz of discovering a new person (a very *promising* new person) and you're walking past elaborate mansions that no doubt house elaborate lives and in the distance there's the bay's steadfast foghorn lament and the occasional cable car clank and you're periodically looking at him and thinking a million different things and then only one thing.

Afterwards he was sweet, offering her tea and control of the remote. But she didn't stay, and she could tell the decision made it worse for him. Immediately she regretted it—"I think I should go," which became the harshest sentence she'd ever spoken—but it was too late. And plus she really did want to go. She suddenly had the postcoital—if you could even call it that—desire to be alone.

It wasn't like this hadn't ever happened before. She had a boyfriend in college who'd been that way, chronically, who'd even read up on the subject to try to increase his stamina. One tactic he tried was to masturbate while watching himself in the mirror and then stop right before he came. Which didn't work. Neither did thinking of sports or Bea Arthur or the ghastly shrunken old woman who replenished the salad bar in the school cafeteria.

She remembered, too, a film appreciation class she'd taken in college, and one of the films they appreciated was *The French Lieutenant's Woman*. According to her professor, the sex scene in the movie represented the most realistic sex scene ever put on film. Why? Because after Jeremy Irons has endured all this unbearable pent-up passion and stinging desire for Meryl Streep, he finally gets his chance to fuck her and he comes in like five seconds and then it's over. He didn't say anything about it having been a while, although that was probably the case, it being Victorian England and all.

Seconds, minutes, an hour—what did it matter really. It was all transitory, over before you knew it, she thought. There were other things to consider.

He never saw himself as the type to videotape the birth of his children, but he'd done it for all three. In fact he became something of a delivery room auteur, jockeying around nurses and orderlies and anesthesiologists to get the best angles, making use of natural lighting, trying to create a Scorcese-inspired gritty realism and edginess. When reviewing the tapes he could see a definite progression in his work, from the first birth to the final one—and it was the final one. There'd be no more kids, they'd decided, no more home movies of blood and birth and beauty. Three was enough.

By then, they no longer lived in The City but in a house in a city (a suburb, that is) where it was okay to say the name. They had neighbors who always waved, gym memberships that did not go unused, financial portfolios with mutual funds that were considered "moderate aggressive." He felt lucky. He was lucky. Sometimes he'd sit in the backyard and soak in the multicolored sunset and pleasantly marvel at the simplicity, the fundamental ordinariness of his life. He'd playfully pat his ebbing stomach and not worry too much about its slow yet determined expansion. He'd see Anna inside the house, knowing that she'd eventually come outside to join him. He loved the waiting, the anticipation of that, knowing that soon he would reach out to touch her and she would touch back. His wife. They'd come a long way since that bar in the Marina. Every year they went there and had a drink to celebrate the anniversary of their first date.

It did not look good. It did not look good at all. He stayed up after she left, unsuccessfully trying to console himself in the numbing whirl of late-night cable until his eyes stung too much and he could no longer watch.

After he awoke later in the morning, he made coffee. While it was brewing, he walked to the café around the corner to get one of those big-ass poppyseed muffins he liked so much. It was all part of his Sunday ritual. He went back to his apartment and read the paper. Twice. Even the travel section. He listened to early R.E.M. and thought about a screenplay that he knew he'd never write. Which was also part of the ritual.

He would see Anna the next day. They worked together. Well, not really together, but at the same company, along with about a thousand other people. They had little work-related interaction, a fact that now made him grateful. They'd struck up a conversation at the office Christmas party a week before. Hence the date. Hence the fuck that was over before it began.

People started dying. Parents, uncles, aunts, coworkers. Even neighbors. Mr. Tillman, for instance, who only a year ago was running in 10Ks and doing Tai Chi at the nearby park (he once showed Aaron a few of the moves, the names of which still stuck with him: "Cloud Hands," "Grasp Swallow's Tail," "Parting Horse's Mane," "Sleeves Dancing Like Plumb Blossoms"). Cancer, of course. You could see how utterly devastated Mrs. Tillman was. Then she died, too. And plus there were the more random middle-aged you-can't-fucking-believe-it deaths: Terry Finkel, car accident; Jenny Blackstock, also cancer, breast; Dave Gingrass, some kind of ski lift accident in Austria. And even kids, teenagers, which was the worst. Through it all, they held each other closer, tighter. They didn't sleep as well as they used to (had they ever slept well?), especially when they knew their two daughters and one son, all full-fledged teenagers now, one about to leave for college and seriously considering becoming a vegetarian, were out, away, doing things they didn't want to know about—but of course they did want to know, and that was part of it, too, the wanting to know and the not wanting to know. It could happen no matter how good you were, no matter how you lived your life. No big revelation here, they admitted, but still, it made you think. How terminally fragile life was, is. It was true: Being a parent changes everything. Your children—they become everything. You make them but then they remake you. And then they leave.

That afternoon she canceled her plans to catch a movie with a friend. Instead she stayed in, writing letters, doing laundry, enjoying the lonely hum of Sunday. The weather was shitty anyway, and what else was new, the fog pouring in as if propelled from a hidden machine. She saw it from her apartment window, pulsing with what seemed to be a secret purpose, the wind bowing back the trees and swirling garbage and dust. (Anna lived three blocks from the ocean, in the Sunset District, where the sun could disappear for weeks on end. Fogville, she called it, which, sure, got to you psychologically, but she'd been desperate to find a place and had unfortunately signed a yearlong lease.) Repeatedly, she tortured herself by playing the night back in her mind. Fuck. She shouldn't have left. Why did she leave? She should have stayed. Everything would have been better if she had stayed. Now there would be this awkwardness, because of that and because of Aaron's, well, brevity. Fuck. Would it have killed her to stay, to lay in his arms and wake up together and then maybe even go out to breakfast and talk about how they've both always wanted a house with a porch and isn't Cormac McCarthy amazing?

The last few men she'd dated were fond of wearing black (and nothing but black) and hanging postcards of obscure Latin American poets on their bedroom walls. So Aaron seemed like such a breath of fresh air. She was just beginning to think she only attracted a certain kind of guy: angst-ridden, distant, unable to accept their anonymity in the world. They usually played in bands or were trying to start bands. Aaron did not play an instrument and he did not quote Rilke. He was from Ohio.

One of her coworkers, Candice from Product Development, had pointed him out to her. "Hottie alert," Candice had said as Aaron approached and then passed them on his way to the kitchen.

Anna usually didn't pay much attention to what Candice said. She was one of those women who Anna had decided to tune out—the kind who were always criticizing other women as too fat, too thin, too slutty, too librarian. But she was right about Aaron. He made her tingle in all the right places.

When she saw him at the Christmas party she hesitated about going over to talk to him. She felt that high school dorkiness that had never left her completely, especially when it came to situations such as this. *Just do it. After all, this could be your husband,* was the whimsical thought that whispered its way into her head, one of those out-of-the-blue aberrations that you think of every now and then because at some point in your life it's going to be true, it will be your husband. *Think of something dazzling to say so you'll have a good story to tell your kids.* Then she laughed to herself. But she didn't have to do anything: He was the one who came over to her. She told herself to remember what song was playing as he made his way toward her, but she got so involved in the conversation, and so taken by his smile (genuine, sexy, a little shy), that she forgot.

There are mysteries, though. He had to admit that. No matter how close you think you are, no matter how truly double-helixed your lives seem to be, you can't know everything. Secrets exist, uncertainties linger. Inevitably there are those things that get lost along the years, that happen and somehow are never picked up again. Like what she said the night of their first date: how she liked it rough. What was that all about? They'd never discussed it, not once in all these years and decades together (there were grandchildren now, the mortgage paid off, a second home in Lake Tahoe, etc.). It had passed. It had simply passed. Although somehow it had haunted them, too. At least it had haunted him. He wondered periodically over the years, whenever there was an especially long silence or when they felt out of sync and foreign to each other, if she was thinking of that, how they'd never talked about it, how she'd liked it rough and she'd never had it rough all these years.

She hadn't wanted to die in a hospital. So they brought her home. They gathered around the bed—their bed—and took turns gently pressing ice cubes to her mouth to moisten the perpetual dryness. "Dad," his children said. "Don't stay up too late. Get some rest, K?" Then he was alone with her. Somehow, he knew. He sat and smelled her smell and remembered as much as he could and watched the final breath of air escape from her lips. Then he kissed them one last time.

All right: He told himself not to dwell on it on the bus ride to work, but of course he did. His only distraction was the woman standing next to him. She was stunning. Occasionally the sway of the crowded bus caused their shoulders to haphazardly rub, which every time it happened caused a pinching little ache to bloom in Aaron's chest. Was she thinking the same thing he was, which was this: What if they started talking? What if he made some comment about the book she was reading (a thick doorstop of a novel, something called *Underworld*) and then that spurred a conversation and it went so well that they exchanged email addresses (safer, better than phone numbers) and that led to a date and another date and isn't it funny how love can strike where you least expect it, like for example a rush-hour bus that smelled of old bread and had no empty seats, and because of this, the lack of seating, they happened to be standing next to each other on a certain day at a certain time…but he didn't say anything and neither did she. And his would-be wife/lover/soul mate/mother of his children got off at the stop before his and he watched her disappear into the downtown crowd, lost forever, his life completely altering in a space of five seconds and then returning back to the way it was. He often had these inwardly dramatic commutes. And Mondays were particularly fertile for such imaginings and longings.

First thing at work, he got settled in for the week, checking his email, returning phone calls, planning out his calendar. He wasn't ready to do any real work yet. He was easing into the day, pacing himself. And all the while Anna hovered in the back of his mind like a bad movie he'd seen a few days ago but couldn't stop thinking of. How would he approach her? What would he say? How would she react? Where was the best place to talk to her?

She worked on the other side of the floor. Her cube had an actual view. You could make out part of the Bay Bridge, the stream of cars and invisible commuters constant, never-ending. People driving no matter what. He still wasn't clear on her job and what she did exactly. Some kind of market research, he thought uncertainly. When time for lunch rolled around he hadn't walked over. He decided to let it go a little while longer, to see how the afternoon developed.

But not long after, he was proofreading a report on the ability of young children to recognize company mascots and logos and then there she was, standing at his cube.

"Hey," she said.

"Hey," he said.

"Have you had lunch yet?"

"No. I was just starting to think about it, though."

There was something in her eyes, her entire face even—a look. A definite look that said yes, maybe something could happen here, it wasn't too late. He told himself not to stare, to continue to use language and stand up and grab his jacket and ask where she wanted to go, what she felt like eating. But the look paralyzed him. He just sat there, happy. At least now there seemed to be, if nothing else, the possibility of the possible. It gave him hope.

ACKNOWLEDGMENTS

These stories originally appeared in various print and online literary magazines during the past thirteen years. So foremost thanks to the editors who championed them and helped bring them into the world for the first time: Roxane Gay; Brock Clarke; Hannah Tinti and Maribeth Batcha; Rob Spillman and Jon Raymond; Linda Swanson-Davies and Susan Burmeister-Brown; Rae Bryant; Adrian Todd Zuniga; Victoria Barrett and Andrew Scott; Ryan Bradley; Celia Johnson and Maria Gagliano; David Cotrone; Matthew Salesses; Steven J. McDermott; Thom Didato; Stephanie Fiorelli, Adam Koehler, and Andrew Palmer; David Lynn; and Meg Pokrass.

Thanks to my agent, the inimitable Michelle Brower, for her unwavering, continuing, and much-needed support and guidance.

Thanks again to Victoria Barrett, a force of nature, superstar editor and publisher, for saying yes and giving this collection a home. Your passion and talent and what you've accomplished with Engine Books—it's all truly inspiring.

Profound gratitude also goes to both the Tin House Writers' Workshop and Squaw Valley Community of Writers.

Lastly, thanks to my family: my mother and my late father; my wife, Maria; and my children, Ethan, Celia, and Henry. Your love and support are behind every word.

And a final tip of the hat to the following folks for encouragement, sympathy, commiseration, and more: Carol Keeley, Amy Wallen, Heather Fowler, Bonnie ZoBell, Alicia Gifford, Roy Parvin, Peter Rock, Andra Miller, Aline Ohanesian, Richard Lange, Jim Ruland, Justin Hudnall (and the entire So Say We All crew), Gina Frangello, Joshua Mohr, J. Ryan Stradal, Stacy Dyson, Sally Shore, and my friends and coworkers at Intuit.

ABOUT THE AUTHOR

Andrew Roe is the author of *The Miracle Girl* (Algonquin Books), which was a Los Angeles Times Book Award Finalist. His fiction has been published in *Tin House, One Story, The Sun, Glimmer Train, Slice, The Cincinnati Review,* and other publications, as well as the anthologies *24 Bar Blues* (Press 53) and *Where Love Is Found* (Washington Square Press). His nonfiction has been published in the *New York Times, San Francisco Chronicle, Salon.com,* and elsewhere. He lives in Oceanside, California, with his wife and three children.